Res... NOAH BOYD
**and his pulse-pounding debut
novel featuring Steve Vail**

THE BRICKLAYER

"Non-stop action and non-stop authenticity . . . a real winner."

Lee Child

"Vail is in the mold of Lee Child's Jack Reacher and Robert Crais's Joe Pike, though more playful than either one. . . . The reader is treated to some of the snazziest, smartest, and often surprising dialogue likely to show this or any season."

Chicago Sun-Times

"Boyd, the author who might have lived some of Vail's adventures, creates consistent tension. . . . Don't miss it, nor the purported sequels to come."

Cleveland Plain Dealer

"Noah Boyd brings his FBI experience to this dazzling thriller. . . . We have a new American hero in Steve Vail."

Patricia Cornwell

"Blistering . . . Enough jolts to create a legion of fans . . . Irresistible red meat for connoisseurs of action thrillers."

Kirkus Reviews

eight FBI-CIA joint investigations, along with their named targets. It had her thumbprint on it."

"Her actual thumbprint?"

"Yes."

"Wait a minute. You mean it was on a *copy* of the list."

"Well, yes. Actually, it was a digital copy of a photograph of the document."

"Then how can you have latents on something that is twice removed from an actual piece of evidence?"

"You're right, you can't. But you could see that each of the pages had been fumed before being photographed. On one of them, you can see the smudge of a print on the lower-right-hand corner. The next page is a blowup of the print. It's a ten-point match with Kate's left thumb."

"I'd hardly consider that *overwhelming.*"

"Steve, she spent two years as liaison with the CIA. There's less than a handful of people who could have put that list together, and she's one of them."

"Wait a minute. Could the examiner see the ridge detail in the latent on the copied document?" Vail asked.

"No, the lab tried to enlarge and enhance it, but the digital quality wasn't good enough. That's probably why Calculus included the page with the blowup."

"If it really is Kate's print, why didn't he provide the actual documents?"

"That was brought up. They thought that he

probably wasn't able to remove the documents, so he just photographed them."

"If he couldn't remove them, then how did the page get fumed for prints?"

"Before the Russians started recording the exchanges, they would sometimes fume documents so that if they could produce the mole's latents on them, they'd have leverage if it ever became necessary."

"But there's no way of knowing for sure that the latent was actually lifted off *that* document."

"I guess not. But there is other evidence."

"Like what?"

"There are a couple of photos of her with a man named Nikolai Gulin, who is a known SVR intelligence officer."

"Any kid with a computer could do that. I suppose the quality of the photos, like the documents, precludes any definitive laboratory examinations."

"Yes, but—"

"You can't believe any of this."

"I don't know Kate that well, but it is hard to imagine. There is one more piece of evidence, though—one that's impossible to ignore. Do you know what spy dust is?"

"The ultraviolet powder that the Russians developed in the sixties or seventies."

"Nobody's supposed to know, but we use it, too. Three months ago one of our sources told us that we had a mole at Bureau headquarters, and the SVR officer who was handling him was this guy Gulin. We put him under intense surveillance for a couple of months, but he was very cagey. Almost every time he went out of the compound, he lost the teams following him. We did manage to get video and photos of him all over Virginia and Maryland, but nothing to prove he was spying. However, he liked this one restaurant, so we put an agent in there as a parking valet. Eventually he showed up and left his car with our man, who planted the dust on the passenger seat and on the carpeting. As you probably know, the purpose of the dust is to track who's meeting with whom by identifying the minute particles being transferred from person to person, which in this case was from car to clothing. Every night for the next month, we swept the Counterintelligence section offices with a UV light, looking for traces of the dust to identify the double agent in our unit. Nothing. It never occurred to us that it was someone from a different division. Once we saw the pictures of Kate with Gulin, Langston got a search warrant. While all her clothes appeared to be dry-cleaned regularly, one pair of her shoes had the dust on them."

"She could have picked that up anywhere."

"The Bureau has taken the technology to the next level. We can now color-code it. For each operation we use a slightly different color. Hers matched up with the Gulin dusting."

"You know this is wrong. Let me talk to her, I'll get to the bottom of it."

"Think about it a minute. If she is being set up, that would mean the Russians gave up three assets to frame a woman who has nothing to do with counterintelligence. Why would they do that?"

"This is so stupid it's laughable."

"Steve, don't get it in your mind that this is some comedy of errors that will eventually right itself. The Department of Justice is charging her with treason. They think they've got enough evidence right now to put her in prison for the rest of her life. And they're going to do their damnedest to make sure they do."

Vail could feel Kalix's words tightening around his heart like an iron fist. This wasn't something he could just run out and fix. For the first time since he'd pinned on the FBI badge eight years ago, he felt the real fear of impending failure.

He took a few seconds so the emotion of the moment could leave him. "Why are you here? You're Langston's man, and I would imagine his making this arrest has made him quite the hero, no matter who it hurts."

Kalix stared at Vail as he contemplated what he was about to reveal. After a few more moments, he said, "Your reputation is that of a man who can keep his mouth shut, and obviously you have no career aspirations. What I'm going to tell you would wreck my career if it went beyond you and me." Kalix looked at Vail for agreement, and the expression on his face said that none was needed.

"Will I do whatever I have to to become an assistant director someday? Yes," Kalix said. "If it means kissing up to Langston or anyone else, so be it. That's the only way it gets done anymore, but I figure once I'm an assistant director, I can do a lot of things right that are now being done wrong. However, my compromises do not mean that I don't know right from wrong, and despite the evidence I just offered, I suspect that Kate is innocent. This is no small wrong. If you hear me agreeing with Langston that Kate is a spy, it's just a means to an end. I have too much time invested, and I've accepted too much abuse, to give it all up now. But between you and me, I'll do whatever I can behind the scenes to help you as long as you promise never to out me."

Vail wasn't convinced that Kalix had been completely forthcoming about why he was there. "Does the director know about Kate?"

"Yes."

The single syllable was delivered abruptly, as some sort of implied message. "Did he send you here?"

"If I had to guess," Kalix said, "I'd say he didn't believe any of the charges either. Of course I'd just be guessing, because the director couldn't get personally involved in a case with the ramifications that this one promises to carry. Especially with how much he likes Kate. You have to remember, however, that the Justice Department has got their teeth into this, so his hands are tied. They won't even let us interview her, because she's so high up in the Bureau." Kalix opened the briefcase he was carrying and took out Vail's gun and credentials, handing them to him. "I would also guess that if he had his way, Director Lasker would want you more than anyone to do something about this."

It was apparent that the director had sent Kalix unofficially to enlist Vail's help.

"John, I'm starting to think that Langston's not

the only one I've underestimated. It looks like you have more than one backup plan."

Kalix smiled. "I've built a career on letting people underestimate me. I am what I am." He started to leave. "Let me know if you need anything."

As soon as the door locked shut, Vail sank down on the marble stair where he'd been standing. Thoughts were rushing through his head at blurred, indecipherable angles. He sat paralyzed, a prisoner of what he'd just been told. After a moment he leaned back, setting his head on the black stone tread above him, looking for the comfort of its hard, cold reality. He closed his eyes and searched his memory, trying to find the image of Kate's face. At least her smile. Then he realized that more than anything he wanted to recall her laugh. Its slightly husky tone, its honest depth. But it wouldn't come to him.

He thought about how confused she must be, how she certainly wasn't laughing at the moment. Was that why he couldn't hear her? Because she couldn't laugh?

Vail bolted upright in anger. Someone had to pay for this. No, *everybody* was going to pay for this.

He turned and ran up the stairs two at a time. In the workroom he let his eyes run along the wall covered with photos and reports. He started pacing back and forth. Since her innocence was not a consideration, only one conclusion could be drawn: Kate had been framed. To clear her he would first have to answer two questions: Who? And, more important, why?

The who had to be the Russians. Calculus, whoever he was, was not a double agent but a front man for the plot to take out Kate. With his mission completed, he probably had disappeared into the maze of his country's bureaucracy. He was probably in Moscow, not being tortured but being decorated. And Vail had fallen for it, all of it.

They had known how to appeal to his ego. He had figured out each of their codes because he was supposed to. If he was really that smart, he would have seen through the plot from the start. There were all those little inconsistencies that he'd explained away so that his answers were the only ones that were acceptable. Ariadne's thread—he had to admit that was the one thing that drew him in. Although its presence didn't make any sense—and Kate had questioned why Calculus would leave a trail of clues if he wanted money for each of the individuals being exposed—Vail had invented a reason so he could feed his own ego.

And now Kate was paying for it.

If he was going to figure this out, the first thing he had to do was disconnect himself from all the emotion of the situation, and that included self-recrimination. He went to the desk and found the file with Calculus's grainy photograph. He pinned it to the wall to remind himself that, although extremely elusive, his enemy was not invisible. He started searching the face for clues of his deception, but of course there were none. Finally he saw the Russian as just another face, his true identity meaningless. The only thing that mattered now was finding a way to destroy his plan.

He got up and went into the kitchen to make some coffee. After filling the pot with water, he started measuring the coffee. As he was about to put in the third scoop, it hit him. He dropped everything and headed for the shower.

EIGHTEEN

THE FLIGHT ATTENDANT ASKED VAIL IF HE WANTED ANYTHING to drink. He smiled absentmindedly and said no. Checking his watch, he looked out the window. They were crossing Lake Michigan, and he could finally see Chicago's ice-covered beaches. The white-and-gray bleakness swept under them, and his thoughts returned to Kate. The one good thing about something as catastrophic as Kate's arrest for treason was that it reduced everything around it to a level of insignificance. Whatever problems there were between them, real or imagined, they would have to wait. Right now her freedom was the only priority.

The thing Vail admired most about money was its way of leading to the truth. Stories could be faked and lies told, but when money was introduced into the equation, honest answers had little choice but to rise to the surface.

While the three-quarters of a million dollars the Bureau had already wire-transferred to Calculus's designated account in Chicago was a drop in the bucket for the Russians, it was still seven hundred fifty thousand dollars American, and chances were that some enterprising soul wasn't going to just let it sit there unclaimed. Even dishonestly gained money had a way of tracing itself back to the truth.

Since he no longer had to worry about Calculus's Chicago "relative" warning him that the FBI was trying to discover anything about the account, Vail could now go to the bank and ask direct questions. Once the plane landed and he collected his luggage, he took a cab to his apartment. He dropped his bags inside and, after spending a half hour clearing the snow off his truck, drove to the Lakeside Bank and Trust in downtown Chicago. It was an eight-story building on LaSalle Street.

Vail flashed his credentials and asked to see the head of security. A few minutes later, a gray-haired man in his late fifties walked toward Vail. Although Vail had never seen him before, his smile was one of familiarity, causing Vail to check the man's hands. He was wearing an FBI ring made from a twenty-five-year service key. Vail stood up and smiled back. "Steve Vail," he said, extending his hand.

"Les Carson." He shook Vail's hand. "I know a lot of the guys from the Chicago office. Are you new here?" There was the slightest edge of suspicion in Carson's voice.

"Can we go somewhere a little more private?"

"Sure, my office." Carson led him to an elevator and then to an office on the third floor.

As soon as Carson closed the door, Vail said, "Actually, I'm out of headquarters, working a special for the director. And it's extremely confidential."

"I'm sorry, Steve, can I see your creds?"

Vail took them out and handed them to Carson. He looked at them for a moment, running his thumb over the embossed seal at the edge of the photo to verify their legitimacy before handing them back. "Why is there something familiar about your name? What other offices have you been assigned to?"

"I was in Detroit for three years, but that was a long time ago."

"That's it. You're the one who was fired during that cop-killer investigation the year before I retired."

Vail smiled. "Sounds like me."

"And now you're back, and at headquarters?"

"The director asked me to come aboard to handle this one case."

"Why would he do that?"

"I did it once before, and it worked out. No one was supposed to know about it."

"What do you do when you're not on the Bureau clock?" Carson asked.

"I'm a bricklayer. I actually live here, on the Northwest Side."

Vail could see that Carson was questioning the plausibility of his background. "And what exactly is it that you need, Steve?"

Vail took out a slip of paper and handed it to Carson. "In the last week, there have been three deposits wired into that account, each for a quarter of a million dollars. I need all the information available about whoever it belongs to."

Carson fell back in his chair. "Come on, Steve, you know that banking information is impossible without a court order. I could lose my job."

"I can get the director on the phone if that would help. It's a matter of national security."

"If you got Jesus Christ himself on the phone, I couldn't help you, and I'm Catholic. I like it here, and I really doubt I'd like being sued. And as far as it being a matter of *national security*, do you know how many times I used that line in twenty-five years?"

"Les, this is extremely important. And I don't have time for a court order. Besides, I can't let the local U.S. Attorney's office know about the specifics of the case." Vail could see that the real problem was Carson's suspicions about him and his story. It was understandable—a stranger was asking him to risk his job on his word alone. He would have been crazy to agree to chance everything for someone he didn't know he could trust. "There's got to be some way you can help me."

The appeal didn't seem to register with Carson. He was studying Vail's face. After a few seconds, he pulled open a file drawer behind him and took out a thick folder. He started flipping through the pages inside. He found the one he was looking for and held it up as though placing it side by side with Vail's features. After studying it for a few more seconds, he looked back at Vail and his mouth curved upward into a smile of discovery. "This is a flyer another bank distributed statewide. It seems last year they had a robbery that went bad, and more than two dozen customers and employees were taken hostage. Then a lone male customer overpowered the two robbers and threw them through the bank's windows. When everything quieted down, the man had disappeared into the crowd. They said he was dressed like a construction worker, and the bank was on the Northwest Side. He was never identified. That's why they sent this out, trying to find out who he is. They wanted to reward him. Why do you think someone would vanish like that?"

"Maybe he didn't want to pay for the windows," Vail said. "Or answer a lot of useless questions."

Carson turned the flyer around to show Vail the surveillance photo of the man who had disrupted the robbery. "You wouldn't know anything about it, would you? What with both of you being from the Northwest Side and in the construction business."

Vail didn't look at the flyer. "Retired or not, Les, you've still got a pretty good eye."

"We heard that when you were fired, it was for doing the right thing, but nobody ever got any particulars. And that bank robbery . . . well, that tells me a hell of a lot more about you than a set of credentials. I assume that any good faith I might show you will be reciprocated."

"Just give me someone to throw through the window."

Carson typed the account number into the computer on his desk. "The balance on that account is zero."

"That's good. What's the holder's name?"

"Donald Brown. With an address in Evanston." Carson started writing down the information.

"Is there a phone number?"

"Yes," Carson said.

"Let's find out if any of this *isn't* phony. Can I use your phone?" Carson pushed it toward Vail and wrote down the number for him.

"Can I ask what kind of case this is?"

"This has to stay right here. The only thing I

can tell you is that it is a counterintelligence matter, at an extremely high level." Vail dialed the number. He listened for a few seconds and hung up. "It's a restaurant. Did this Brown withdraw the money himself?"

Carson queried the computer again. "No, all three deposits were wire-transferred out of here the day they were received."

"To where?"

Carson hit another key. "That's odd, it doesn't show. That information has to be listed."

"Does someone have to authorize those transfers?"

"Yes," Carson said. "But the data can't just disappear. Let me get ahold of our IT guy." While Carson made the call, Vail wondered if he hadn't run into another dead end.

He felt something he wasn't used to—panic. What if he couldn't figure this out? What if Kate went to prison? How could this be happening? He thought about what she must be going through, the confusion of being one of the top law-enforcement officials in the country and then, the next moment, a prisoner. And even if they were able to clear her, was her career over? Her competence was already being questioned because of that ridiculous suicide rumor. How could she recover from this? She must be going crazy right now. At least he was able to do something about it to keep his sanity.

He hoped she would realize that he was working on it. If only there were some way for him to get word to her that he was, but that might prove just as difficult as tracing the three-quarters of a million dollars that had seemed to vanish from the bank.

Carson said, "He's going to trace everything through the computers. I told him to make it a priority, but it'll be at least an hour. Come on, I'll buy you lunch."

WHEN THEY RETURNED, Carson called the computer analyst back. Almost immediately he started writing on a pad of paper. "Okay . . . Okay . . . Really? That's odd. Can you trace that? . . . Okay, thanks, Tommy." He hung up. "All three transfers out of the bank were authorized by employee code '13walker13.' And it looks as if the same person wiped the transfer information from our computer."

"What's his name?" Vail asked.

"It doesn't matter."

"Why?"

"That was the user ID for one of our vice presidents who retired six months ago and moved to Arizona. His access to the system was never canceled. Someone got ahold of it and used it."

"So the Bureau sent three-quarters of a million dollars to this bank and there's no way to track where it went."

"The IT analyst says he doesn't think so, but he's going to keep at it. I have to apologize, Steve. Security at this bank is my responsibility, and obviously I've got some work to do."

"Don't disembowel yourself just yet. The people involved in this investigation are very smart and have gone to a great deal of trouble and possess unlimited resources. If it's any consolation, I've been made a bigger fool than anyone. We'll just have to get creative."

"How?"

"Whether you're after the lowliest of thieves or the president of the United States, what's the one tactic that rarely fails?" Vail said.

"I don't know, what?"

"*Follow the money.* Is there a phone somewhere I can use in private?"

"Use mine. I'm going to go find out how this happened."

"Actually, if you could, leave that access in place. I think I know a way to use it."

After Carson left the office, Vail picked up the phone and dialed John Kalix's number.

NINETEEN

AT A FEW MINUTES BEFORE EIGHT THE NEXT MORNING, VAIL walked into Les Carson's office and asked, "Your people ready?"

"I just talked to Tommy. They're locked onto that account. In fact, the deposit won't move out of here until he personally releases it."

"And if 13walker13 accesses it, we'll be able to trace it to whoever is using the password?"

"To whatever computer is being used in this building, yes," Carson said. "This *must* be a big case. One phone call and you get them to send half a million dollars that's just going to disappear into . . . who-knows-where."

When Vail had called Kalix, he told the deputy assistant director he wanted the half million dollars they had promised Calculus for the final double agent to be wired to the same Chicago bank first thing in the morning. Kalix had argued that was in effect tantamount to giving the Russians half a million dollars more for framing Kate. He feared that when it got out, which the Russians would make sure happened eventually, it would be highly embarrassing for the FBI's Counterintelligence Division.

Vail said, "It's the only way to track whoever set up Kate."

"As much as I want to help Kate, I simply cannot authorize the release of that much money, knowing that it's probably going to wind up in the hands of the Russians. We've already given them three-quarters of a million dollars."

"Actually, we're not going to give them anything. When you send the money, we're hoping that their man here will transfer it to wherever he sent the other payments. I'll have the bank put a twenty-four-hour hold on whatever bank it's transferred to. Once it's transferred out of here, we'll immediately be able to determine the bank and the account number it's being sent to. Then we'll invalidate the transfer from here, and the money will be sent back to the account you forwarded it from. Zero loss."

"Steve, it sounds like there are too many things that could go wrong, and then we're out five hundred K."

"John, take a few minutes to meditate over this. Even consult your 'higher authority.'"

"Uh . . . oh, yes, yes, I could do that." Kalix realized that Vail was hinting at contacting the director for approval.

"Good. Call me back when you're done mulling it over." An hour later Kalix called and told him the payment would be ready to be sent first thing in the morning.

Vail said to Carson, "Let me call Washington, Les, and then we're on."

While Vail made his call, Carson stayed on the line with the bank's IT manager. After a few minutes, Carson hung up and said, "Okay, the half a million just arrived."

Vail asked, "Right now, who can check on the account's balance?"

"There are dozens of employees who have general access to account information, depending on their jobs."

"And how many people can actually order transactions involving that account?"

"It takes a completely different level of clearance to move money out of it, generally vice presidents and above. You said these people are smart. Aren't you afraid they won't fall for this?"

"That's always a possibility, but we have one thing going for us: *five hundred thousand dollars.* That's halfway to seven figures. The best thing about greed is how quickly it melts even the smartest person's IQ."

"As many employee embezzlements as I handle in a year, I should get that little bon mot framed." Carson checked his watch. "I don't suppose there's any way to tell how long this'll take."

"No, I'm not even sure this person is still working here." Vail considered the possibility that with Kate in custody the Russians might have pulled their man out of the bank. But if he was still checking the account, no matter what he'd been told to do, the amount of money just transferred into it might be too great a temptation. "If he is, I would think he wouldn't check that account any more than once a day—otherwise someone might notice. So if you've got work to do, Les, don't let me keep you from it."

Carson took a stack of papers from his in-basket

and started initialing them. Vail picked up the newspaper from the small table next to him and began reading it.

A little before noon, Carson had lunch brought in, and the two men, evidently believing that a watched pot would never boil, found other things to talk about. When they were done eating, Carson went back to work, placing a call to Tommy to make sure everything was still being monitored. Vail started on the crossword puzzle.

At a few minutes to five, Carson noticed that Vail had fallen asleep. As quietly as possible, the security chief started clearing his desk. Suddenly the phone rang, and Vail's eyes snapped open. The two men looked at each other. Carson straightened a little and picked it up.

"Yes." He listened for only a moment before disconnecting the line. "The money's being transferred right now." He dialed a four-digit extension. "I want everybody to the basement immediately. Someone's on the computer terminal there. Whoever it is, I want held until I get there." Carson pushed the phone back into the cradle. "He used the same password as before." Both men were moving toward the door. "We have one computer terminal in the basement, mostly for storage inventories."

Once they were in the hall, Vail said, "Will the stairs be quicker?"

"No, the only access is by elevator. You need an override key." They ran to the elevator, and Carson pounded the button repeatedly. Finally the car arrived.

Just as the doors opened to the basement, the two men heard three quick gunshots.

Vail drew his automatic and ran toward someone yelling for help. In a large room stacked with boxes, one man in a suit was on his knees tearing open the shirt of another man who'd been shot in the stomach. Carson, directly behind Vail, said, "Those are both my men."

Vail raised the muzzle of his weapon upright. "Who was it?"

"That guy Sakis from accounting, Jonas Sakis. He went out that way." He pointed to a corridor beyond the computer station.

The security man's wound was now exposed, and Vail looked at it. He checked the man's face for signs of shock. Carson was already calling 911. Vail took out a handkerchief and placed it over the wound, then pulled the kneeling man's hand onto it. "There, use that much pressure. Watch him for shock. Les, where does that lead?" Vail nodded at the corridor the shooter had disappeared into.

"It's a dead end. There's no way out."

The man on his knees said, "Except the old railroad tunnel."

Vail remembered the news story from the early nineties, when an engineering miscalculation had caused the Chicago River to seep into the sixty miles of tunnels, forty feet below the downtown area. They had been built to move freight under the downtown area in the early 1900s. With typical Chicago buoyancy, a city that had been rebuilt after the Great Fire, the incident was referred to as the Great Chicago Leak. "The old freight tunnels?" Vail asked. "I thought those were sealed."

"Our door is, but that's the only thing back there."

As Vail started in that direction, Carson said, "Steve, you'd better wait for the cops."

"Either of you have a flashlight?" Vail asked.

The kneeling man pulled one out of its carrier on his belt and handed it to him.

"I've got a feeling that door is no longer sealed," Vail said.

Without turning on the light, he followed the corridor until it turned right. As soon as he looked around the corner, he could see the door. It was made of steel and was three times the width of a room door. And it was open.

Before entering, he stood and listened. He couldn't hear anything, so he leaned his head in. It was dark except for the ambient light from the bank's storage space. The tunnel itself was concrete—floor, walls, and ceiling—six feet wide and maybe seven feet high. He snapped the flashlight on and then quickly off so he wouldn't provide a lasting target. Thirty yards in was a concrete bulkhead with a gate, a lock and chain lying on the deck next to it. Without turning the light back on, Vail started toward it, his Glock raised to eye level. *What is it with me and tunnels?* He flashed back to the electric train tunnel in which he'd been buried alive during the Los Angeles case. *Maybe I should wait for the cops.*

Then he thought about Kate. When he'd been an agent, after a while there was a gamelike quality to working cases. They rarely took on any real urgency, any real consequence. If he failed on one, there were dozens more to take its place, and he still got to go home and watch the game that night. But he was getting just one shot at this, and it was ahead of him in the tunnel. He couldn't risk losing the only lead that could free Kate. Whatever might happen to him was no longer a consideration.

When he reached the gate, he turned his light back on. Once he determined that the shooter wasn't on the other side, he picked up the lock. It appeared to have been cut with a bolt cutter—and, from the surface rust, not recently. That meant the tunnel was a planned escape route, so Vail didn't have to worry about being ambushed, because the shooter wanted to put as much distance as possible between himself and anyone foolish enough to pursue him. At least it sounded like a good enough theory to let him rationalize throwing caution to the wind. He turned on the light and broke into a trot.

Another hundred yards ahead, he found a second bulkhead with the padlock cut away. Vail noticed that the odor in the tunnel was becoming more pungent, and he thought he could detect the slightest trace of methane. The air was stale and felt heavy in his lungs. He tried to measure his rate of breathing to see if his lungs were requiring more oxygen, but he wasn't feeling light-headed, so it probably wasn't going to be a problem. Besides, the shooter had apparently been through here before without a problem.

After a few more minutes, Vail found himself at a three-way fork in the tunnel. Stopping at its intersection, he turned off his light and listened. There wasn't a sound. After turning the light back on, he could see he was standing in a couple inches of water that had accumulated because the floor at the intersection was an inch or two lower where the old switching tracks had been removed. In the left-hand passage, the floor was dry. The same in the center. The floor of the right branch revealed some partial footprints left by the shooter's wet shoes. Vail took the right branch and after ten feet turned around and compared his tracks against those of Sakis. The rate of drying was difficult to judge, but the early tracks weren't that much different. He was still close enough for Vail to catch.

Seventy-five yards later, Vail came to a right turn. It was impossible to tell what direction he had traveled in, but he thought it was initially south and now possibly west. As he was about to make the turn, he heard the sound of metal on metal. He peeked around the corner and saw another bulkhead with a steel gate. The man he'd been chasing, illuminated by his own small flashlight, was busy working on something attached to the ceiling of the tunnel. Vail drew his weapon and carefully inched forward.

When he got to the gate, he saw that it was chained and locked shut from the other side, separating the two men. Carefully, Vail pushed his Glock through the bars, aiming it at Sakis. He couldn't be sure, but it looked as if three linear-shaped charges had been attached to the ceiling in a triangular pattern. Each one had wires coming down from it to an electrical detonator. Vail snapped on his flashlight and said, "I guess I'm a little early."

Sakis looked up, unruffled, keeping his hand on

the detonation box. "You are. I thought maybe I lost you at the fork. If not lost, at least delayed."

Vail could hear a slight accent in the man's speech but couldn't tell its origin. "Why don't you carefully set the box down and come over here and unlock the gate?"

"You are evidently not a student of game theory. What you are proposing is a zero-sum game—all the advantage goes to you while I lose."

"I'm fairly certain that zero-sum games are exactly what gun manufacturers have in mind. I believe their collective motto is 'If you have the gun, you win.'"

"But this detonation box makes it a non-zero-sum situation."

"Actually, this is more like a game of brinkmanship. We're each promising to cause the death of the other to gain an advantage. I could kill you with one shot, and if I did, you would flip that switch and set off the charges on the ceiling."

"True," Sakis said, smiling. He raised the box in front of his face so that Vail wouldn't have a clear head shot and end Sakis's life before he could throw the switch. "Do you know where we are standing right now?" When Vail didn't answer, he said, "Directly under the Chicago River. If the blast doesn't kill you, the tunnel will flood instantly and you'll drown. It's too far back to the bank to outrun it. Too bad the gate between you and me is locked, because the way out for me is about twenty yards ahead. Of course, you can't get to it. Unless you think you can shoot that lock off, but that's a heavy-duty lock I put on it. I guarantee a handgun won't dent it."

"It'll dent you. If you even twitch, I'll empty this magazine into you."

Sakis smiled calmly. "There is one solution. We could each go our own way, you back to the bank and me out through the exit. A draw."

"And what's to prevent you from coming back and setting off those charges once I'm around the corner?" Vail asked.

He laughed. "Nothing at all. But I suspect you know that if we both stay here in this stalemate, the police will eventually find us, and I'll lose. Or maybe we all will. So I guess I'll just have to take a chance your marksmanship isn't that good."

Vail said, "You're ten feet away, and I have a couple of full magazines. Do you really think anyone's that bad a shot? Maybe I'm the one who should take a chance that those charges won't go off."

Sakis smiled. "They're triple-primed. They'll go off."

Vail laughed and then in a theatrical voice said, "What we have here is a failure to compromise." The man looked at him uncomprehendingly. "*Cool Hand Lukesky?*" Still there was no indication of understanding from Sakis. "I guess they don't allow American prison movies in Moscow. Even the southern road gang is better than the gulags."

Finally Sakis smiled as if he knew something Vail didn't. "Exactly what compromise did you have in mind?"

"I'll back up five feet from the gate. Then you come up to it and set down the detonator at one side. With me that far back, it would be too difficult a shot to risk hitting you through the bars. You stand

at the other side as far as possible from the detonator, take the key to the gate, and throw it as far
down my part of the tunnel as you can. By the time
I retrieve it and come back to the bulkhead, you'll
have enough time to make it to the next turn and
out of range. Once I get the key and can open that
lock, you'll be gone and I'll be five minutes behind
you. Then there'll be no reason to set off the explosives."

Sakis considered the proposal. Evidently this FBI
agent had forgotten the gun he had shot the guard
with. It was now tucked behind his back. "You have
to lower your gun."

"Okay," Vail said, dropping his arm to his side.
Then he stepped back the agreed-upon distance,
never taking his eyes from Sakis's.

Sakis figured that once he threw the key behind
Vail, the agent would have to turn his flashlight
away from the gate and in the other direction down
the tunnel. If he did glance back momentarily, he
would be watching the box, making sure Sakis was
not moving toward it. As soon as he fully turned to
search for the key, his own light would silhouette
him, and Sakis would shoot him in the back. Then
he could trip the detonation timer before making
his escape.

Sakis took the detonator and set it down along
the wall about a foot from the gate, so Vail couldn't
reach through and disarm it. He then moved to the
opposite wall, dug a key out of his pocket, and
held it up so Vail could see that it was a padlock key.
"Okay?"

"Toss it."

Sakis threw the key as far as he could, at least ten feet past the agent, who was now casually leaning against the wall. Vail gave him one last careful glance. Then he swung his flashlight around, and its beam glinted off the key on the concrete floor ahead. Vail turned the light back onto Sakis and the detonation box. "I've got a feeling it won't be too long before we meet again." He turned and started toward the key.

Sakis reached behind his back and carefully drew his gun. As he raised it, Vail dropped into a crouch, pivoted, and fired. The bullet tore into Sakis's throat.

Vail hadn't forgotten about the gun. He knew that Sakis would use it if Vail created a scenario in which Sakis could shoot him in the back. The ploy was the only way he could separate him from the detonation box. Vail had hoped to shoot up through his throat and sever his brain stem, not only instantly killing him but also paralyzing him so the switch could not be thrown. The odds of making the shot were astronomical, but he had no other choice. The bullet had missed by almost two inches.

Although fatally wounded, Sakis was not paralyzed. He sank to his knees and fell forward, reaching for the box. Vail started to squeeze off another round but realized that it was too late when he saw Sakis's index finger trip the switch.

He ran up to the gate as Sakis rolled off the box, his eyes vacant with death. In the darkness Vail could see the red LED display. It read 2:58 . . . 2:57 . . .

Vail ran back and retrieved the key. At the gate again, the lock was on Sakis's side and the chain was thick and difficult to maneuver. The bars on the sides of the gate were narrower than the gate itself. Vail's hand barely fit through. With his right he grabbed the chain on his side and manipulated it to bring the lock closer to his left hand. 2:43 . . . 2:42 . . .

Carefully, he tried to place the key in the keyhole, but the lock was large and had a spring-loaded metal cover to protect it from debris and weather. He pushed the cover back with the key and just about had it seated when it slipped from his hand and fell to the floor. 2:07 . . . 2:06 . . .

Dropping down to his knees, he shoved his hand through the bottom of the bars, but it was well out of reach. 1:59 . . . 1:58 . . .

Vail stripped off his belt, then his shirt and T-shirt. There was a small puddle of water under the gate; he soaked his T-shirt and then tightened his belt around it. 1:42 . . . 1:41 . . .

Threading them through the bars, Vail threw his shirt at the key, holding on to the end of the belt. His first cast landed on the key. Slowly, he drew it back to him, the weight of the water keeping the key under the shirt as it was pulled toward him. 1:30 . . . 1:29 . . . 1:28 . . .

Finally he was able to grab it with his fingertips. He delicately inserted it in the lock—this time it seated fully. He tried to turn it, but it wouldn't move. Vail then realized that Sakis had thrown him the wrong key, maybe one for a gate ahead.

Vail's laughter bellowed down the tunnel. "If I had a hat, I'd tip it to you for making that switch." He glanced at the timer: 1:14 . . . 1:13 . . .

The closest part of Sakis's body was his foot. Vail reached through the bars and could get just two fingers on his trouser cuff. He pulled it to the bulkhead. Working his way up Sakis's leg, he eventually had the entire body against the gate. He pulled part of the other man's suit coat through the bars and patted the pockets, hoping there was another key. He couldn't feel anything through the cloth. 1:01 . . . 1:00 . . . 0:59 . . .

He grabbed at Sakis's left trouser pockets, front and back, pulling them close enough to pat them. Still nothing. 0:47 . . . 0:46 . . .

Using only his fingertips, Vail grabbed Sakis's belt and pulled it toward him to roll the body partially over. Finally he was able to feel the right front trouser pocket. There was a set of keys in it. But he couldn't roll the body over any further, because it was against the bars, and the pocket, although he could grasp its opening edge, was facing away from him. He took out his lockback knife and slit the material open, exposing a key ring.

From behind him Vail could hear voices and footsteps. The cops. And it sounded like there were a half dozen or more of them. He looked at the timer: 0:31 . . .

Vail took the ring and was relieved to see a key similar to the one Sakis had decoyed him with. He stood up and, holding on to it with both hands, worked it into the lock. It turned. He pushed the gate open. 0:24 . . . Vail ordered himself to stop looking at the timer.

The device appeared to be basic. Timer, power supply, electrical blasting caps wired to the three shaped charges attached to the concrete ceiling. Vail wondered if the timer had been booby-trapped, but then he reasoned that he was never supposed to get to it. So he took the first blasting-cap wire, doubled it over, and stuck his knife's blade into the loop and pulled. The wire severed cleanly. Quickly, he did the same to the other two. The first cop's flashlight finally came into view. Vail looked at the timer and watched as it counted down from 0:11. "Plenty of time," he said out loud. He watched as the readout continued, which it would even if the bomb was defused. When it was about to go to 0:00, he closed one eye, squinting at it. The display went black.

"Let me see your hands," the first police officer said.

Vail raised them and then heard Les Carson say, "That's all right, he's the agent."

Vail stepped back through the gate, partially closing it. "Sorry, guys, there's explosives in there. I think they're defused, but you'd better get someone down here who knows what he's doing."

A sergeant walked forward and peered through the gate. "That the shooter?"

"It was."

"Why was he trying to blow a hole in the ceiling? To escape?"

"We're under the Chicago River. Actually, he was trying to kill the rest of us," Vail said.

Les Carson came forward and looked at the body. "Yeah, that's Sakis. At least that's the name he gave us."

Vail straddled the body. Remembering the fake passports and escape plans that Petriv had been supplied with, he started going through Sakis's pockets. There was no wallet, but in the suit coat Vail found a grainy photograph. Recognizing the background, he realized that it had been taken in Washington. But it still surprised him.

It was a photo of himself.

TWENTY

JOHN KALIX WATCHED VAIL COME THROUGH THE GATE AFTER the flight back from Chicago. He searched his face for any indication that he had just killed another man, but he couldn't see any. "How you doing, Steve?"

"Good. Any word from Ident on Sakis's prints?"

"There's no record. And that security director at the bank, Carson, forwarded his résumé. He started checking it and said so far the work history appears completely phony."

"He was a lot more educated than a bookkeeper should be," Vail said. "When we were nose to nose, he started discussing game theory with me. It's scary to think the Russians plant one of their people in a Chicago bank for that length of time just to handle wire-transferred funds. Makes you wonder how many more there are out there."

"Maybe the Russians didn't plant him there only for the Calculus scam. Maybe they were washing money through the bank, or something else. I'll open a case on it and have Chicago check it out. Some Russian operations have been around for twenty years. There's probably some that have been in place since the thirties, and we just haven't uncovered them yet. They're not like us—they've got that long-haul mentality."

"Maybe you should let them know the Cold War is over."

"It's all about technology now. They want to steal as much of it as possible. It converts directly into their country's economy."

"Did you get the court order for the bank here? What's the name of it?"

Kalix tapped the breast pocket of his suit coat. "Right here. Northern Virginia Trust in Annandale. When do you want to go out there?"

"Kate's still in custody—what do you think?" Vail increased his stride, and Kalix hurried to keep up.

Once they were in the car, Kalix said, "After your not-so-low-profile shooting, I had no choice but to tell the assistant director that you'd been reinstated."

Vail laughed. "Sorry I missed that."

"I wish I had. If I hadn't implied that it was the director's idea, I'd be working the Migratory Bird Act in the Bronx right now."

"Why don't you just give me the court order? I can take it from here if you want to go repair some bridges."

"I think I'll hang in there a little longer."

"I'd almost admire your courage if the director weren't your ace in the hole."

Kalix smiled. "Actually, he's more like a royal flush in the hole, so I'm with you—unless, of course, he becomes disenchanted with you. Then I'll be calling for your head," he said. "I assume this bank account will also turn out to be a phony?"

"I'd be surprised if it were legit, but it's our best shot right now."

AS THEY WALKED through the bank lobby, Vail started scanning the faces of the employees, wondering if one of them was another plant by the Russians, put there to move money. Kalix led the way to the manager's office and flashed his credentials, introducing himself and Vail. Once he did, he handed the bank officer the court order and pointed out that it instructed him to provide the mentioned records and that any disclosure regarding the FBI's visit would be a violation of federal law.

"Sure, I understand." After reading the document, the manager started typing at his desktop computer. He took a pen and wrote down a woman's name, her phone number, and an address in Alexandria. "This is all the info we have on the account holder. There was a transfer of five hundred thousand dollars to it yesterday, but that was canceled first thing this morning. The balance is zero." He slid it across to Kalix, who glanced at it and handed it to Vail. The manager went back to the court order. "What are these three other dates you're requesting?"

Vail said, "They are additional transfers made from the same Chicago account. We're not sure whether they came to your bank, but if you could check, we'd appreciate it. They were each a quarter of a million dollars."

After a few more minutes on the computer, the manager said, "They weren't sent here."

Vail said, "Again, if someone asks, it's best that we were never here."

"I understand," the banker said.

As they left, Vail said, "I'll drive," and got behind the wheel.

"I assume we're going to Alexandria."

Vail glanced over at him, indicating that an answer wasn't necessary. "Can you get that name checked?" Kalix pulled the radio mike from its mounting, and Vail put his hand on top of it. "I don't think you want that name going across the air, even if the channel is scrambled."

"You're right. I wasn't thinking." Kalix dialed his cell phone and after giving some instructions waited a couple of minutes before saying "Thank you" and hanging up. "Nothing on the name, but according to the utility check the address is good."

"Let's go take a look at it." Vail glanced at him as if trying to decide something about him. "Are you carrying a gun?"

Kalix blushed a little. "For the first time in years."

"Really? Why now?"

"I guess for the same reason I'm helping you instead of fully protecting my flank."

"Which is?"

"Do you remember when you got your appointment to new agents' training, what an adventure this all was going to be? How daily life was going to go from ordinary to fantastic? That's what I thought. Then I got to the field. The first two years in WFO were spent working wiretaps. I had no choice but to go into management to get out from under the earmuffs. In seventeen years with the Bureau, I haven't had one of the days I signed up for." He looked at Vail to see if what he was saying was registering. "This may be my only chance to be something other than the man in the gray paper suit."

Vail laughed. "It sounds like you're ready to do something stupid."

"Is that a bad thing?"

"Do you really think I'm the person to ask?"

For the next twenty minutes, neither of them said anything. Finally Vail pulled over and motioned to a house in the distance. "That's it there."

Kalix sat up. "It doesn't look like much."

"One of the little lessons I've learned during my stay in Washington is that the Russians prefer their ambushes to be isolated."

"You think this is a trap?"

"A trap or a dead end. Unfortunately, a dead end isn't going to help us." Vail opened his cell phone and dialed the number that the bank manager had given them. He held it away from his ear so Kalix could hear. After three rings a woman with a heavy Eastern European accent answered. "'Allo."

"Is Clarence there?" Vail asked.

"No one that name here," she said, and hung up.

Vail put the car in gear. "So far so good."

"What's good? You're not going to the house, are you?"

"I thought you wanted to do something stupid."

"Shouldn't you get some help?"

Vail smiled at him. "I've got some. When I go

to the front door, you take the back." Kalix had his hand on his automatic, unsure whether he should draw it or not. "It's okay, John. Haul 'er out."

Kalix gave him an embarrassed smile and eased the automatic from its holster.

They pulled up in the driveway, and as both men got out, Kalix hurried to the back of the house. Vail walked up the three stairs onto the front porch and knocked hard on the door's window. He didn't wait for an answer, knocking again even more loudly. After a third time, there still was no answer. He yelled back to Kalix, "I'm going in!"

The house was a small one-story structure, and Vail could tell by the exterior construction that there was no basement. The door wasn't locked, so he pushed it open, drawing his own automatic.

Someone had tried to rehab the drab interior cheaply. The floors were unfinished plywood, and the walls were mostly unmatched paneling. Like most houses that old, it was a basic rectangle with low, seven-foot ceilings, which were clogged with spiderwebs. To the right, through a doorway, Vail could see into the kitchen. There were two partially eaten carry-out meals on the table, which was a card table flanked by two folding chairs. Two beer bottles sat next to two empty glasses. At the bottom of one of the glasses, Vail could see small bubbles hugging the inside, indicating that whoever had been drinking beer had been gone no more than a few minutes. Since Vail and Kalix had been sitting outside that long, it meant that at least one person was still in the house. Not able to remember how to say "good afternoon" in Russian, Vail yelled *"Dobroie* utro!" and then, in English, an even louder "Good morning!" There was no answer.

Vail backed out of the kitchen and into the entryway. Straight ahead was what looked like a living room, although it was difficult to say without any furniture. Carefully, he walked into the room, his face brushing against more cobwebs. He caught a glimpse of Kalix out the back window, peeking in. Vail tried the door on the right side of the room, but it was locked. He moved from in front of it and knocked. *"Dobroie utro."*

Again there was no response. The dead-bolt lock on the door looked brand new and out of place on an interior door. Across the room, directly opposite, was another door, leading to the left rear of the house. It was ajar and without any sort of visible lock on it. Cautiously Vail moved to it and pushed it open. At the top of the door, he noticed that some of the cobwebs that hung from the ceiling were matted against it, indicating that it had been closed recently. As he peeked around the jamb, he could see that the room had probably been a bedroom, with a surprisingly large closet crudely constructed in one corner.

Vail pulled his head back and leaned against the wall. Someone was in the house, and as far as he could tell, there were only two places to hide: in the locked room across from him or the closet in this bedroom. The fact that the one room had a locked door made it the more logical. The door, a hollow-core laminate, would not present any problem to kick in, but he wanted to eliminate the closet first. Once he determined that it was empty, then he could call Kalix in and they wouldn't need to watch their backs as they went after the more likely target. With the two of them working in tandem, they could safely make entry into the locked room.

Raising his handgun to eye level, Vail went into the bedroom and moved quietly to the closet. Standing at the side, he grabbed the wooden knob on its door and pulled it open. When nothing happened, he looked in. It was empty, except for a full-length mirror that ran from the top to the bottom. What a bizarre place for a mirror, he thought.

He turned to go but then realized something that hadn't immediately registered when he looked inside. At the top of the mirror, as on the door of the room, the ceiling cobwebs were matted against it. At the same moment, he heard a tiny metallic click that he'd heard a thousand times before. He spun around 180 degrees and fired four shots into the mirror. It exploded as the body of a man fell through it, a silver automatic dropping from his hand.

The cobwebs that were caught against the top of the mirror were in a triangular pattern, indicating that it opened on a hinge, catching them in a pattern similar to the one above the room's door. Vail could now see the secret compartment behind it. The click he'd heard was the gun's safety being released. As he stooped to pick up a piece of the mirror, there were a half-dozen shots fired from behind him. He dove to the side and rolled over, looking for a target.

In the doorway was a second man, slumping to the floor. Vail could see Kalix looking in through the window he'd just shot through. "Steve, you okay?" he shouted, his adrenaline apparently still pulsing.

"Yeah, come around to the front." Vail went to the man whom Kalix had shot and verified that he was dead. Holstering his gun, he walked back to the closet and picked up a piece of the mirror, examining it.

Kalix came in at a trot. "You really are okay, right?"

"Are *you* okay?"

"I heard some shots, and when I looked in the window, I saw this guy coming up behind you ready to fire, so I opened up. He is a bad guy, isn't he?"

Vail smiled. "Not anymore." He held up the mirror fragment. "Two-way glass. I should have realized that the closet was deeper, but the mirror was meant to distort its depth."

"Any idea who they are?"

"I would imagine they're guys who get their paychecks in rubles." Vail looked up at Kalix, who continued to stare at the man he'd just killed. "You want to go wait in the car? I'll take care of searching these two."

"No, no, I'm all right," Kalix said. "Should I have yelled for him to surrender or something first?"

"This isn't exactly a surrendering bunch. If you had yelled, I'd be dead." Vail rolled over the body of the man he'd shot and started going through his pockets.

"They were here to ambush us?" Kalix said.

"They were probably here to ambush me. But now that you've killed one of them, maybe they'll give you equal consideration next time. With Kate in custody, they probably figured I'd be alone."

"Why you?"

"Apparently they're finding me to be a bit of a nuisance. Sakis had a photo of me in Chicago."

Kalix studied Vail's face, looking for fear. "Doesn't that bother you?"

"Never look a gift horse in the mouth."

"A gift horse?"

"I must be moving in the right direction, otherwise why try to kill me? I just have to figure out exactly what I've been doing to upset them."

Kalix chuckled. "Better you than me."

"You're about to have your own problems."

"I am?"

"Somebody needs to call your boss and bring him up to date."

The smile disappeared from Kalix's face. "Who would have thought that keeping you from getting killed would be a bad thing?"

Vail laughed. "Is that a rhetorical question, or do you want an alphabetical list?"

Kalix squatted down next to the second man and started searching him. He pulled a cell phone out of the man's pocket and turned it on. Staring at the screen, Kalix said, "Whoa."

"What?"

Kalix turned the phone so Vail could see it. On the screen was the same photo of Vail that had been found in Sakis's pocket. Vail took it from him and scrolled through the phone's options. "It was sent last night around eleven thirty."

"They must have figured that this would be your

next stop. And where one man failed yesterday, they felt two would succeed today."

Vail pushed a couple more of the phone's buttons and handed it back to Kalix. "There's the number the photo was sent from. Think you can get someone to break it down?"

Kalix started dialing his own phone. "What do you think it is?"

"I'm hoping it's a link to whoever is behind all this. But I'm not betting anything over a dollar. Someone's trying awfully hard to make sure Kate stays in prison."

TWENTY-ONE

AFTER MORE THAN THREE HOURS OF INTERROGATION BY THE Annandale police and Bureau agents, Vail and Kalix headed back to Washington and the off-site. "Come on in. I'll buy you a beer," Vail said.

They walked into the workroom, and Kalix motioned toward the wall. "You and Kate sure covered a lot of ground on this."

Vail came back from the kitchen and handed him a beer, cracking open his own. "A lot of it is the tracking information from the phone you guys gave Calculus."

"It looks like a lot more than that." Kalix opened his beer and took a small sip as his phone rang. "John Kalix."

He went over to the desk and got ready to write. Then he dropped the pen and straightened up. "There's no way to trace it at all. . . . You're sure? . . . Okay, then your best guess. . . . Okay, thanks." He disconnected the line. "That was one of the techs. The phone company has no record for that number."

"How can that be?"

"After being told it didn't exist, he called the number and got a busy signal. So, since the number was active, he called a contact who handles covert government 'contingencies,' as he calls it. Best guess is that it's CIA. It's a clearing number. If a source needs to leave a message, he leaves his code name so it'll get routed to his handler. But it's mostly used for dry-cleaning traces, a dead end in the trail. Say you wanted to make a pretext call, like you did today before we went into that house, but you didn't want anyone to be able to trace it. You dial the covert number plus a code and then the number you want to call. It's then put through like a regular call. You can send photos, or text, or anything else you can do with a regular line. And if anyone tries to track it, you get the answer we just did. It doesn't exist. If you call it, it rings busy unless you enter the code."

"How do Russians get access to a CIA tool like that?" Vail asked.

"Maybe one of their moles sold it to them. Once you pay a source for something, you generally feel it belongs to you. But the problem is, we can't even determine if it was the CIA who gave it up. Other agencies know about things like this. We figured it out. Even if we did find out it was CIA, there are hundreds of employees who probably have access, authorized or unauthorized, to that number."

Vail said, "Instead of this getting clearer, it seems like we're getting further and further from any answers."

Kalix didn't answer. He was back at the wall, studying the charts. Vail could see that something had caught his attention, so he sat down on the couch and sipped his beer, waiting.

Finally Kalix turned around. "I haven't told anyone this, but ever since I was up here with Langston and saw these charts and realized that's how you found the three spies, I had a duplicate set made for me from the file. I've been spending a lot of time studying them, especially while you were in Chicago. I really wasn't making too many connections until we came up with this CIA number. See if this makes sense: We know that someone has framed Kate. Most likely the Russians. But why Kate? She's not in counterintelligence, at least not now. And she was only exposed to that work twice. Once in Detroit when you were there and she was supervising a squad covering the Middle East, right?"

"Right."

"And her only other CI assignment was when she had liaison here at headquarters with the CIA. So now with this phone number probably being the agency's, that's twice we've had the CIA come up. The big question is, how do the Russians and the CIA fit into a frame of Kate?"

Vail said, "I don't know."

"I can think of one possibility. Let's say the Russians have a highly placed source in the CIA. But there's a problem. Somewhere in his travels, he ran into Kate Bannon at the wrong time. Maybe he was doing something he shouldn't have been, something that might compromise him, something that, coupled with an upcoming event, might click together for her. So this CIA agent and his Russian handlers now have a problem. Maybe they decide to kill her, but they can't just assassinate her, because the investigation would never cease, and once solved the Russians would be considered more evil than they were during the Cold War. So they decide to make it look like an accident. I assume you know about her 'suicide attempt.'"

"The director told me. He thought it was as ridiculous as I did. If your theory is right, maybe the Russians were trying to make it look like she took her own life. She did think she was slipped something. And once that didn't work, maybe an accidental death would work just as well. Like when we had to rappel off that building and the rope was rigged to look like we'd died trying to escape the fire. We're sure the Russians orchestrated all that. But then they tried to kill just me when I went after Petriv."

"Maybe they thought she'd be with you," Kalix said. "Up to that point, you two had been into everything together."

"So then the Russians went to Plan C, to provide proof that she is guilty of treason and get rid of her permanently. Which was their final, fail-safe plan all along. It's hard to believe that the entire Calculus ruse was set up to protect somebody in the CIA who's spying for the Russians," Vail said. "But it's the only thing that makes sense out of all this." He went to the wall and started examining the charts.

Kalix asked, "Do you think Calculus's movements have something to do with it?"

"I don't know. But Calculus is the key to this, and thanks to these we know everywhere he went until he disappeared. Maybe they are the answer."

Kalix stepped up next to him and glanced at the maze of photos, charts, and notes covering the wall. "Do you want me to stay and help?"

"No, why don't you go get some sleep, and we'll start fresh tomorrow. I'm going to go to bed myself. Call me first thing in the morning." Vail smiled crookedly. "If you dare."

After Kalix left, Vail lay down on the couch and stared at the wall. It was too far away for him to read, but that was good, because he was starting to wonder if there were any larger patterns he was missing. He started to retrace Kalix's theory through the different sections of the information on the wall, but then his burning eyelids slid shut.

VAIL FELT SOMEONE tap him on the leg. "Steve." He opened his eyes and was surprised to see Lucas Bursaw standing over him. "I know it's late, but I saw your car outside and the lights on."

Vail checked his watch. "Late? It's almost five A.M."

"The computer geeks finally finished that Volume Shadow Copy query you suggested. They found fourteen files on Sundra's laptop that had been deleted in the thirty days before she disappeared." Vail sat up, and Bursaw handed him a thick stack of pages with the contents of the files printed out.

Vail let his thumb riffle through them. "That's still a big haystack."

"I was up most of the night with it. There are five of them that look like she was working pretty hard."

"And the other nine?"

"She found nothing illegal and closed them, giving her a reason to delete them."

Vail thought for a second. "So if she was still working on the other five, why delete them?"

"That's why I'm here. They were all wiped from the computer the day she disappeared."

"Sounds promising. Have you taken a look at them?"

"Yeah, but there's nothing that I can see. What do you say we check them out and see if we can get someone to flinch?"

"Luke, I've got something to tell you. Kate's been arrested."

"What!"

Vail then proceeded to tell him everything, from being picked up at the hospital New Year's Eve to his trip to Chicago to the shoot-out the day before.

"Kate? A spy? Even the Bureau can't be that stupid."

"You're right, it's the Justice Department. And they're low-keying everything about it. She hasn't been formally charged. I guess they're hoping if she spends enough time locked up, she'll tell all."

"Don't they have to arraign her?"

"Special provisions have been made. They can hold her for up to ten days before letting her see a judge."

"Whatever misguided thing you're about to do, I'm in," Bursaw said.

"I appreciate it, Luke, but—"

Abruptly Vail got up and walked away as though Bursaw wasn't there. He went to the workroom wall and picked up a blue highlighter. He drew a streak through one of the entries, and then, after searching a few more seconds, he drew the blue slash through a second, then a third. He picked up the phone and dialed Kalix's home number. "Get over here."

Vail hung up and said to no one in particular, "Why didn't I see this before?"

KALIX KNOCKED ON the front door, and Vail went down to let him in. "What is it?" he asked Vail.

"I think I found something. Come on."

Once they were upstairs, Kalix noticed Bursaw. "Who's this?"

Vail introduced them. "Luke is at WFO, and he and I go back to Detroit. He's been deputized and given the appropriate death threats."

Kalix shook Bursaw's hand. "That's good enough for me. . . ." The deputy assistant director's voice trailed off with a trace of apprehension.

Vail pointed at the newly highlighted entries on the wall. "On three different occasions, Calculus went to the exact same coordinates. A place that it doesn't make sense for him to go even once."

Kalix studied them for a moment. "What is it?"

Vail went over to the computer and moved the mouse, lighting up the monitor screen. The Bureau satellite was online. "Bryn Mawr Park. About a five-minute drive from . . ." Vail moved the cursor as it traced the map along Route 123 and then Chain Bridge Road.

Kalix took a step closer to the screen. ". . . CIA headquarters at Langley."

"And that means what?" Bursaw asked.

Vail looked at Kalix and then at Bursaw. "I have no idea."

Kalix said, "It means we're one step closer to . . . What time of the day were these three contacts?"

Vail picked up a file and started making notes. When he finished, he handed Kalix a slip of paper. "At 10:03 A.M., 1:42 P.M., and 10:48 A.M."

Kalix turned around and smiled at them.

"What?" Vail asked.

"All three are during working hours. Have you ever been to Langley?"

"No."

"You can't get in or out without swiping your ID."

"So the CIA will have a record of people leaving headquarters on those dates, around those times. That's great, but I doubt they'll be willing to share that with us."

"I have a good friend over there. We went to law school together. And he's in Personnel."

Vail pushed the phone toward Kalix. He picked it up and dialed.

After Kalix hung up, he said, "Maybe by this afternoon. He has to sneak around a little to do it. He's going to call me at the office. As you probably heard, I had to promise him first notification if something comes up on one of theirs." Kalix got up to leave.

Vail asked, "Where are you going?"

"Back to the office. I have a meeting I can't miss. I'll call you as soon as I hear anything."

After he left, Vail went back to the wall and started scanning it. Finally he turned to Bursaw and said, "Let's get out of here for a while. What do you say we go cover some of those leads on Sundra?"

"You sure you want to bother with that now?"

"I need something to do. Let's go make some people nervous."

FOR THE NEXT three hours, the two men fell into an old rhythm developed during three years of friendship and working together in Detroit. They complemented each other well, picking up on the familiar nuances of criminal behavior, which weren't much different whether they were in D.C. or Michigan.

The first stop was a Middle Eastern travel agency. Sundra's file did not document why she was investigating them, but once Vail and Bursaw started interviewing the owner, they discovered that he had a large marijuana-growing operation in the building's basement. They decided that someone had flagged the premises based on the inexplicable electrical consumption caused by the massive lighting system used.

The next one turned out to be an identification mill operated out of a residence. The individual in charge of the operation provided forged driver's licenses and car titles for a hundred dollars apiece. He had been arrested years before and received probation. When he told the two agents that his lawyer said he would probably be continued on probation if caught, Vail and Bursaw felt satisfied that he had nothing to gain from Sundra Boston's disappearance.

"Two down, three to go," Vail said as they got back into the car. "Lucas Bursaw, tell us who our next contestant is?" Before Bursaw could answer,

Vail's cell phone rang. It was Kalix. Vail listened for a few seconds. "Okay, we'll meet you there."

Bursaw said, "What's up?"

"We're going to have to put this on hold. John has that list of CIA employees."

TWENTY-TWO

WHEN THEY GOT TO THE OFF-SITE, JOHN KALIX WAS PARKED outside waiting for them. They went upstairs, and Kalix handed Vail the list of names, along with their photos.

"Names and photos—you must have something on this guy."

"Actually, I do. Like I said, he and I went all the way back to law school. We were pretty close. We were out one night having a few cocktails, and he spotted a source of his in the bar. I guess he thought I'd be impressed, so he introduced me to the guy. The source was horrified that someone would see us, and he tried to leave. My friend caught him outside and started slapping him around. The asset made a stink, and I wound up lying about it to a couple of their internal grunts. He was absolved, and now he's paying the bill."

Vail made a quick count. "Nine. That's not bad. Have you run the names through indices?"

"Personally searched them myself. Nothing."

"We have one advantage right now—surprise. If we confronted them, we'd lose that. Besides, from the moment these people decide to start spying, they're constantly rehearsing their answers to any questions about their loyalty. Anybody have any ideas?"

Kalix and Bursaw both shook their heads.

"Sorry, boys, there appears only one thing we can do," Vail said. "We've got to show the photos to Kate."

"How are you going to do that?" Kalix asked. "They won't let anyone from the Bureau near her."

"John, this is where we separate the temporary help from the truly self-destructive."

Kalix laughed. "Talk about making something sound irresistible."

"Come on, how many FBI agents can say they helped a federal prisoner escape?"

"If you mean without becoming a federal prisoner themselves, I'm going to guess zero."

ALFRED BEVSON, THE United States Attorney for the District of Columbia, sat at his desk rereading a newspaper article regarding a shooting in Annandale the day before. The facts seemed deliberately vague, and that, coupled with the participants' being two unnamed FBI agents and two suspected East European illegal immigrants, made him wonder if it had something to do with the Kate Bannon case. His secretary buzzed him. "Yes."

"There's an attorney by the name of Karl Brickman on the line. He insists on talking to you."

"Just tell him I'm in a meeting and I'll call him back."

"He said he was representing Kate Bannon."

"What?" Bevson swore under his breath. The

FBI must have leaked her detention. "Okay, Claire, put him through."

Bevson knew that the Bureau was upset with him for cutting off their access to her, but by his own admission their director was too close to her to let the FBI stay actively involved. The last thing Bevson needed right now was more bad press. They'd been all over him recently on the issue of the escalating crime rate in the District, and there were rumors that the present administration was about to replace him because of it. The Bannon case was supposed to sweep all that into obscurity, and it probably would once its depth was reported to the world.

If they fired him anyway, the important thing was having a soft place to land. If he could publicly manipulate his role in this treason case against an FBI higher-up, the big firms would be calling. Washington loved a good spy story, and there were firms that would hire him for no other reason than to hear the insider gossip. But all that would be diluted if the FBI was going to leak every detail of the case, as they usually did when it was to their advantage. For once he was going to beat them to the punch. But first he would have to put out another one of their well-placed brush fires. "This is Al Bevson, can I help you?"

"Karl Brickman. I see from your online bio that you went to Georgetown Law, so I know you were taught the concept of due process. Apparently you think there's some exception to the rule when it's an FBI agent who's been charged."

"I'm sorry, who is your client again?"

"You want to know who my client is? Put on the

six o'clock news tonight and you'll find out. It won't matter which network—they'll all be carrying it."

"You told my secretary it's a Kate Bannon."

"And you've had her in custody for three days without taking her before a judge or a magistrate. In civilized countries that's called an abduction."

"Mr. Brickman, if we were holding someone as you have suggested and you went to the media, be advised you could be violating national security."

"If you consider what you've done to Kate Bannon as being in the best interests of national security, then it needs to be violated."

"There's a lot you don't know about the case."

"Apparently there's a lot you don't know about prosecutorial malfeasance. I've already contacted the assistant director at the FBI who has jurisdiction over this case, William Langston, and given him the same option I'm about to give you. If I don't meet with my client within three hours, in three hours and one minute I start making calls to the media."

The door opened, and Bevson's secretary came in and handed him a note.

Assistant Director Langston, line 3. Urgent!

"Mr. Brickman, can I call you back?"

"No, you can't. In exactly three hours, I'll be at the FBI building. If I'm not immediately taken to see my client, you know where I'll be going next." The line went dead.

Bevson punched the line-three button. "Al Bevson."

"Bill Langston. I'm the Counterterrorism AD. Did you get a call from a lawyer named Brickman?"

"That's who I was on the phone with. Who is he?"

"I made a couple of calls after he threatened me. His practice is primarily criminal. A one-man firm, and he is not a media hound. I guess that's why I've never heard of him, but the word is he's the last guy you want to have coming at you."

"How the hell did he find out about Bannon?"

"I was going to ask you. You're the one who won't let us near her, remember?"

Bevson said, "Someone might think a call to a lawyer would be a good way to get even with us for that."

"It's just as likely that someone from your side did it. You're the one with all the lawyers. Maybe you should ask around and find out if any of your people know him personally."

Bevson knew that was true. These days, "leaking" was an act of self-indulgence. "It's out there now, so it doesn't matter. What do you think we should do about it?"

"This cannot get to the media. Until we can secure some cooperation from Bannon or we can be sure no one else is involved, we've got to keep this buttoned up. Every time there's the least hint of someone's being identified, that person is murdered, and each time it's arranged so it looks like the Bureau had a hand in it. How about this: Have a couple of marshals bring her over with one of your assistant prosecutors, and we'll give her the full-court press one more time before Brickman shows up. He told me he was coming over at three o'clock. In fact, how soon can you get her here?"

"I'm guessing an hour or so."

"Good, I'll line up our best available interviewers, and they can take a shot at her."

"Can my man sit in?"

"The best interviews are done one-on-one, but if she breaks, your man can draft up the formal statement, and then you'll be able to spin it any way you want."

"I don't care who gets credit, I'm just—"

"Please, Al, save it for the press conference. Just have them call my extension when they bring her in—2117."

KATE SAT IN her cell at the Correction Treatment Facility in southeast Washington. It was where all female prisoners arrested in the District of Columbia were housed. The cell had a window, but it had been covered over with sheet metal, which made the cement-block cubicle seem that much smaller. She had never experienced claustrophobia, but the moment they shut the door, she felt a sense of mild suffocation, as if the air were being secretly drawn out of the space, or at least the oxygen level was being manipulated to a level that would not allow logical thought.

A concrete bed with a thin mattress, a seatless toilet, and four pale green walls were all she'd seen for the last three days, except for the matronly guard with a lifeless face who brought her meals twice a day.

Kate was well aware that this sensory and social isolation had a purpose. It was to soften her up. But it wasn't the austere surroundings that were having an effect. It was the three days. Three days without someone rushing to her cell, throwing open the door and telling her that a terrible mistake had been made, something she was waiting for even now.

When arrested, she was confronted with the evidence: the photos, the prints, and the dust on her shoes. She had to admit that if she'd been on the other side of the table, she wouldn't have been interested in listening to the unprovable denials that she presented in her defense.

All of a sudden, she realized she was crying. Not full sobbing, but she could feel the weight of her tears working their way down her cheeks. She couldn't remember the last time she cried, probably when her mother had died. She suddenly realized just how scared she was.

Even if she were somehow miraculously cleared of the charges, her career would be destroyed. It had been hanging by a thread ever since her "attempted suicide." Legally, people could be found not guilty, but within the pedantic confines of the Bureau she would never be judged innocent.

Isolated like this, with no apparent end in sight, she couldn't help but worry that somehow this case would be proved at trial. The evidence wasn't airtight, but conversely she had absolutely nothing to refute it. The only thing that was keeping her sane was knowing that Vail was out there somewhere. If anyone could unravel this, it would be him. But there was a very good chance he didn't even know she'd been arrested. She let out a short, hysterical laugh. It had been part of their plan to keep these arrests out of the public eye. And the last time she saw Vail, she'd sided with the Bureau against him. Then she was told that he had again been stripped of his credentials. Because she'd told him there was no possibility of a personal relationship between them, he'd undoubtedly left Washington by now, on his way to Florida, where no one knew how to contact him. Luke might have been able to track him down, but of course Luke wouldn't know about her arrest either.

Her thoughts were broken by the sound of the cell door opening. She stood up in anticipation of rescue, but it was the same female guard, her face stony as usual, who set down a metal tray and left.

ASSISTANT UNITED STATES Attorney Fred Bisset had been put in charge of Kate Bannon's prosecution the day she was arrested. The case against her had been damning, with one exception: She'd helped gather the evidence against the other spies that had led to her unmasking. But in all probability, Bisset theorized, she was trying to find any evidence against her and destroy it before it came to anyone's attention. Despite everyone's best efforts, she had steadfastly maintained her innocence. Then, an hour ago, he'd received a call from the United States Attorney himself, ordering him to get her over to FBI headquarters ASAP.

That was why he was now walking into the J. Edgar Hoover Building with Kate, who was flanked by two U.S. Marshals, one male and one female. Bisset had made the decision that if she were handcuffed and brought into her place of employment, any remaining secrecy about her status would be destroyed. And that would certainly preclude any admissions she might be about to make.

Bisset went to the receptionist, showed his identification, and told the woman that they were expecting him at extension 2117. She dialed the number and said, "Someone will be right down."

Within a minute Lucas Bursaw got off the freight elevator that was away from the mainstream traffic and held the door open. He was careful not to show any recognition of Kate, hoping to send her the message to do the same. "Mr. Bisset!" he yelled over to the group. "We can take this one!"

They walked to the elevator, and as they got on, Bursaw moved to the back of the car. "We're going to room 349." He leaned forward slightly and pointed at the buttons. "Can you press the third floor, please?" As the female marshal hit the button, Bursaw slipped a small, folded piece of paper into the back of Kate's waistband.

When the door opened on the third floor, Bursaw said, "It's to the right. Number 349."

Once the four of them were in the room and seated, Bursaw said, "Can I get anyone anything?" When they declined, he said, "I'll be standing by in the director's suite if you need anything. The extension there is 1207." He wrote down the number and handed it to the AUSA. Then Bursaw closed the door behind him.

Immediately Kate said, "I'd like to use the ladies' room before we get started."

Bisset looked at the marshals and pointed at the female. "Okay, but she'll be going inside with you."

"Fine." Kate led the way, and when they got there, the female marshal went inside and checked it for avenues of escape while the male stayed with the prisoner. When she came out, she said, "No other doors or windows." The male nodded. Once the two women were inside, Kate went into the stall and shut the door. She took out the note and read it: *Tell them you'll talk, but only after you apologize to the director in person*. It was in Vail's handwriting. "About time, bricklayer," she whispered.

"What?" the female marshal called in to her.

"Sorry, nothing." She flushed the note down the toilet and came out.

Once they were back in the interview room with Bisset, Kate, for the first time, took a good look at him. He was in his early thirties, and even though he was severely balding, he kept the remaining patches of his hair closely cropped. Without paying much attention to his attempted banter on the way over, she remembered his using the line "I'm no fool—I graduated from Stanford Law School."

"What time is it, Fred?" she asked.

Though he hadn't noticed it before, he now detected some warmth in her attractive face. He quickly checked his watch and said, "It's almost two."

Kate examined him more closely and decided that anyone who would cut his hair that short, drawing attention to the uncomeliness of male pattern baldness, was someone who probably had an inability to interpret common social cues, especially those of rejection. Book-smart with absolutely no people skills, something she suspected was going to be to her advantage. "I'm sorry, where did you say you went to law school?" She was careful to ask the question with just a hint of sarcasm.

"Stanford. I thought I mentioned that."

"I guess you did. I'm just a little tired. Bet you were the top of your class." This time the sarcasm was as obvious as she could make it. She glanced at the two marshals and could see that they were experienced enough in handling prisoners that all conversations around them were no more than white noise.

"I made law review," he answered, trying, but failing, to sound humble.

"It's pretty obvious how smart you are. Me, I just *thought* I was smart. I'm tired of all this. I'd like to make a statement."

Bisset straightened up, appearing as though he hadn't been paying attention and wasn't sure what she'd said. "You want to make a statement?"

"Can't get anything past you law-review boys. Yes, I'd like to make a statement."

"Now you're being smart." Quickly he dug into his briefcase and pulled out a pad of legal paper. "Where would you like to start?"

"I'd like to start with an apology to my director, Mr. Lasker."

"As soon as we get your statement."

"I see him first or there is no statement."

"You're the prisoner, Miss Bannon."

"This offer expires in five seconds . . . four . . . three . . ."

Bisset grabbed the phone on the desk. "Okay, I'll get him on the line."

"No. This has to be in person. Face-to-face. He's been very good to me, and I owe him that much."

Bisset stiffened, and it took a moment for him to realize what had to be done next. He dialed the number that the black agent had left him. Bursaw answered, "Director's office."

"Yes, this is Assistant United States Attorney Bisset. Miss Bannon has had a change of heart and is willing to make a statement, but first she says she needs to talk to the director."

"About what?" Bursaw asked, as skeptically as possible.

"She wants to apologize to him."

"I don't know if he wants to talk to her."

"She says she won't make a statement until she can."

"Hang on." Bisset heard the line go on hold, and then, within a minute, Bursaw came back on. "He said he'll see her. Let me get another agent, and we'll come down to get her."

Ten minutes later there was a knock at the door, and when the marshal opened it, Luke Bursaw was standing there, and behind him was Steve Vail. Bisset said, "You'll bring her right back here after she's done with the director." It wasn't a question but an order.

"The director says she's got five minutes and

that's all," Bursaw said. "So you'll have her back in no more than twenty minutes."

The elevator car that Kate, Vail, and Bursaw got into had a half-dozen other employees in it, so they didn't speak until they were out the front door of FBI headquarters. Kate said, "It took you long enough. I almost forgot what you looked like, Stan."

As they walked toward their car, Vail watched her profile in the clear winter sunlight, her breath clouding the cold air in rhythmic streams. She took a deeper, stuttering breath, her freedom evidently registering. "Actually, it's Steve."

"I assume that since you've turned me into an escaped federal prisoner, you still haven't figured out who's responsible for setting me up."

"After looking at the evidence, I'd say your innocence is questionable."

"Then why did you break me out, Stan?"

"I thought by now you'd be ready for a conjugal visit."

"Suddenly prison isn't looking so bad."

They got to the car, and Bursaw climbed in. Kate grabbed Vail and turned him around, kissing him fully. "Thanks, bricklayer." She got in.

"Let's see if you're thanking me when this all goes south."

Suddenly her smile was gone, and her eyes started to well up. "Sorry, Steve, but all this is scaring me."

"You'd be a fool not to be scared." He put his arm around her. Then he took out his credentials and showed them to her.

"I thought you had to give those up to Langston."

"And who's the one person in the Bureau who can rescind my being fired?"

"The director?"

"So you've got friends in high places. Plus, you're innocent. Or so I'm told. I promise you you're not spending another minute in jail." Then Vail filled her in on his trip to Chicago and the shoot-out he and Kalix had been involved in. He told her about his phone call to the United States Attorney, with him posing as her attorney and Kalix playing the telephone role of his boss, William Langston.

"Kalix did all that for me?" she said.

"What about me?"

"How many times do I have to thank you? You've really gotten needy while I've been in the big house."

"But unlike John I'm not trying to suck up to the director," Vail said.

"That's a great way to talk about a guy who saved your life."

"Yeah, well, I'm sure you'll find some way to get even with him for that."

AUSA FRED BISSET checked his wristwatch again. It was now exactly twenty minutes since the two agents had left with Kate Bannon, and it was starting to seem a little too long. He again called the extension the black agent had given him for the director's office. It rang six or seven times before a female answered it. "Hello."

"*Hello?* This is Assistant United States Attorney Fred Bisset. Let me speak to the director, please."

"The director? This is the employees' break room. Let me get you back to the switchboard."

When the operator came on the line, Bisset again identified himself and asked to be put through to the director's office. He waited a moment, then heard, "Director Lasker's office."

"This is AUSA Bisset. Could I speak to the director, please?"

"I'm sorry, he's in New York for a regional conference."

"Then can you transfer me to Assistant Director Langston?"

"I'm sorry, he's with the director."

TWENTY-THREE

AS BURSAW DROVE CAUTIOUSLY THROUGH THE CITY'S streets, Vail asked Kate, "Do you have any idea what this is about?"

"It's all I've been thinking about since they came for me. I have no idea."

"Could it be something to do with the CIA?"

"The CIA? Why them?"

"It's better if you answer my questions first."

"Okay. Let's see, the CIA. The only real contact I've had with them was when I had Bureau liaison with them. I was over there almost every day. More there than at headquarters, actually. But I think I already told you about that."

"Ever have problems with anyone there? Any suspicions about anything?"

"No, not that I can remember."

Vail took out the nine photographs of the CIA employees that Kalix had given him and handed them to her. "Do you know any of these people?"

Kate went through them slowly, carefully studying their features, knowing that work ID photos, due to the regimented posing and general lack of quality, can be more difficult to identify. When she finished, she shuffled back and picked out one. "He's the only one I know. Myles Rellick. He was one of my contacts there."

"Anything about him that didn't sit right with you?"

"Not really. Do you think he's involved in this?"

Vail explained about finding the CIA safe phone number, Calculus's three Bryn Mawr Park visits, and how Kalix had narrowed the times down to the nine men in the photos. "You must have seen something, or at least they think you did."

"I don't know, the guy was beige wallpaper. Nothing sticks out about him."

"You don't need to dwell on it. Just let it roll around in the back of your head for a while. Maybe something will surface."

"Where are we heading?"

"Thanks to Luke, we have a safe place to stay."

"Didn't Bonnie and Clyde say that once?" Kate said.

Bursaw said, "My sister is a history professor at Georgetown, and right now she's on a sabbatical, in Portugal. That's her area of expertise. She has an apartment near the school. There's a car. I'm kind of in charge of maintaining both. She won't be back until May for a summer course she's teaching. It's just a one-bedroom, but it's well stocked with food. And she's about your size if you need clothes."

"What about all the files and information we have at the off-site?" she asked Vail. "Won't we need that?"

"It's all in the trunk. And we took photos of everything on the walls. I don't know if they're going to go public looking for you—and me, I suppose, since it won't take long to figure out who helped you. But I don't think they can announce to the world that you escaped, seeing as how they refuse to acknowledge that you'd been arrested. Lasker's got Langston out of town for a couple of days, leaving Kalix in charge of counterintelligence operations, so the Bureau won't be burning a lot of manpower hunting for us. And Luke should be cool for a while, because if they do try to identify Unknown Black Agent Number One, they'll start at headquarters. No one knows about us being friends. We should have a couple of days before there's any type of full-court press."

Bursaw turned off Rock Creek Parkway onto Pennsylvania Avenue and then turned up Twenty-eighth Street. Three blocks later he pulled up to a small apartment building. "This is it," he said, getting out and opening the trunk.

Inside his sister's residence, Bursaw put the box containing the files on a desk in the living room and handed Vail the keys. "You're now officially in charge of them." He pointed at a large fish tank with a couple dozen disinterested tropical fish swimming around. "The car is a powder blue VW Bug. It's parked in the garage. The key card to get in and out is over the visor."

"Are you going somewhere?" Vail asked.

"I've got to go home, change, and go to the office. I hope you're right and they won't be looking for me. As soon as I put in an appearance and see if there's any general alarm for you two, I'll be back to give you a hand."

"Thanks, Luke," Kate said, and kissed him on the cheek.

Vail walked him out. "Is there an access code for your sister's answering machine?"

"Good idea. We can leave each other messages on it if you go out. It's 777."

"I'll call Kalix and let him know what Kate said about the photos. It looks like Myles Rellick is our best bet, but I have no idea where to start. We can't do surveillance, or a wiretap, or even search his financial background. This fugitive stuff isn't as easy as it looks."

"I'm sure you'll figure something out. Especially since it's for Kate, her being such a good *friend* and all."

"I told you, it's complicated."

"The best things always are."

When Vail came back in, he found Kate looking through the bedroom closet. "Sorry we didn't have time to get some of your clothes."

"I'd rather wear three-day-old clothes than a nice crisp prison uniform."

"Anything there?"

"I'll find something," she said. "I'm sorry I got emotional in the car."

"Any CIA epiphanies yet?"

"Not yet, but I'm too tired to summon up any real memory. I'm going to take a shower and get some sleep. You could probably use a couple of hours yourself. You look beat."

He smiled at her mischievously. "I could use a shower, too. This place looks like it would have a limited supply of hot water."

"That's good," she said in a playful tone, "because it sounds like you could use a cold shower."

After a couple of seconds, Vail said, "Kate, I'm

sorry. This is all my fault. The whole thing was a setup, and you're paying the price. I was so smug figuring out those puzzles. 'Ariadne's thread.' I should have picked up on something."

"Like what? Everything was falling into place."

"Like their killing the moles, and just as we got to them. They knew just when to kill them—because they were sending us to them. That should have registered with me."

Gently she took his hand in hers. "I should be terrified right now, but— No, that's not right. I am terrified. But with you here I know this is going to end well. So *please*, don't stop being you."

"Probably the smartest thing you could do right now is be worried."

"Well, bricklayer, I'm so worried that I'm going to sleep. You probably should, too."

Vail picked up one of the pillows from the bed. "Maybe you're right. I'll stretch out on the couch and see if I can't nod off as soon as I call John."

A FEW HOURS later, Kate walked into the living room, her face still full of sleep. "Tell me it's New Year's morning and I just had a bad dream."

Vail sat up on the couch. "I don't suppose you dreamed about who would do this to you."

"Nothing. As far as the CIA people at Langley, I was kind of a ghost. Float in, do a little paperwork, say hello to a few people, and float out."

"You've got the Russians on you. You're a threat to somebody. I know you supervised security work in Detroit, but that was the Middle East, right?"

"Right."

"When was the last time you worked the Russians?"

"Never. When I rotated out of Detroit, I went to OPR for a year, and then I was a unit chief in the Counterintelligence Division, but it was an administrative position, the liaison with the CIA. I had a desk at Langley, but it wasn't like I was there sixty hours a week."

"Where else were you assigned?"

"After my CIA stint, which was about a year and a half, I got tapped to go to New York as an ASAC. But just before I was to leave, the director called me in and told me he wanted me to be the deputy AD in the general criminal division. So I haven't been in counterintelligence for almost two years. And then it had nothing to do with the Russians."

Vail was silent, staring back at her without seeing her. He was quiet longer than usual. "Did you handle any assets when you were there?"

"No, I haven't seen an informant since I was a street agent," she said.

Vail just shook his head.

There was a knock at the door, and then they heard a key in the lock. Bursaw walked in, carrying a large pizza box.

"How's the manhunt going?" Vail asked.

"Not a word about it at WFO and nothing on the news. I went by the off-site, and there are a couple of guys sitting on it. They look like marshals."

Vail said to Kate, "Then they're on your apartment, too."

Bursaw opened the box and pulled off a piece of pizza. "So what's the plan?"

Vail pulled off a slice and handed it with a napkin to Kate. "I wish I knew."

A few minutes later, there was another knock at the door, which caused everyone to stop talking. Vail peered out the peephole. It was John Kalix. He came in carrying an oversize briefcase. "I think I found something," he said.

Kate stood up and hugged him. "Thanks for everything, John, except for maybe keeping the big galoot here alive."

"I'm kind of new at all this, but I'll bear that in mind next time."

"What's going on at headquarters?" Vail asked.

"I wish you could have seen that AUSA when he came storming into my office. He was making all kinds of threats until I asked him, with as incredulous a tone as possible, why his boss would accept a lawyer's identity over the telephone. He said the entire hoax was perpetrated by FBI agents in the FBI building and that he was going to get to the bottom of it. Needless to say, he didn't ask for any Bureau manpower to hunt down the wily Katherine Bannon. My sources tell me he has two two-man teams of marshals looking for you, and that's all."

"As long as Luke isn't identified as part of this, we should be safe here," Vail said. "You said you found something."

Kalix took a portable DVD player out of his case. "While I was sitting around trying to look nonchalant after you and Kate disappeared, I got an idea. I started thinking about the spy dust that's part of the evidence against Kate. Since we know she's innocent, it means that the Russians must have collected it when we used it on that SVR intelligence officer, Nikolai Gulin. And maybe it isn't a coincidence that he's also the one in the photo with Kate. So I ran him through everything we have. Remember I told you that he was very elusive, but that we did have photos and videos of him taken during surveillances a couple of years ago? When I reviewed everything, I found this. It was taken at the Fredricksburg Antique Mall, which is far away enough from Washington that it was a good spot for a meeting or a drop. Anyone ever been there?"

Kate said, "I was there once . . . I don't know . . . a couple of years ago, visiting a girlfriend of mine who had just moved to Fredricksburg from Colorado. It's kind of a fun place. They had some interesting stuff."

"Then you know people don't go there without some interest in antiques, even if it's casual. According to the surveillance log, Gulin never went into one shop or even looked in a window. It is, however, a place where it's not easy to follow someone, which is probably why he chose it. As I said before, we had information that he was working an FBI agent. In this video it looks like he could be meeting with someone, but we couldn't be sure because we lost him within minutes of this being shot. There was never any real effort to identify the second individual."

"Why not?" Kate asked.

"This doesn't leave the room." He looked at each

of them to make sure they understood. "Langston reviewed the matter, watched the video, and made the decision, almost arbitrarily, that the second individual had nothing to do with Gulin." Kalix set the player down in front of Kate and pushed the Play button.

Everyone crowded in behind her and watched. The secreted camera bounced as it followed the Russian. Finally the target stopped and turned around. Kalix hit Pause. "That's Gulin," he said. "Ever seen him before, Kate?"

She studied the image for a moment. "Not that I remember."

"Now watch when he stops in front of that bench." Kalix hit Play once more. Gulin's back was again to the camera, and a man walked up next to him, his back also to the camera. Then the man turned around, and they could see his profile. Kalix reached over Kate's shoulder and hit Pause. "What do you think, Kate? Do you recognize him?"

She leaned forward. "It does look like Rellick. Maybe if I saw him move around a little more."

Kalix hit Play again. The individual turned his back to the camera and appeared to be discreetly talking to Gulin. Then he casually looked to his right and abruptly turned to his left. He lowered his head and said something brief. For an instant the camera jerkily panned over to the right, trying to film whatever it was that had caught his attention. "I think it is him," she said. Both men on the screen then separated and walked off in different directions.

Kalix hit the Stop button. "I spent an hour looking at his photo and then at the video. It's hard to tell if you don't know the person, but it looked like a match to me."

Kate replayed the video a couple more times. "I'm almost positive that's him," she said. "Does this mean I'll be cleared?"

"It would be better if we could be positive it's him. What do you think, Steve?"

Vail didn't answer but instead reached over and backed up the DVD. Then he pressed the Slow Motion button. When the camera panned over to what had distracted the individual believed to be Rellick, Vail hit Pause. Kate gasped. "That's Jennifer. And me." The woman she had identified as the friend she'd been at the mall with was near the edge of the frame, and half of Kate was next to her. They'd been all but invisible when the video was run at normal speed. "He must have seen me, and that's what spooked him."

"Then all this was to protect Rellick," Kalix said. "He thought you could put him with his Russian handler." He laughed. "All this to get rid of you, and you never even saw him. He must be a very good source for them to go through all this to protect him."

"But why now?" Kate asked. "That was a couple of years ago."

Vail said, "Maybe it was your momentary appointment to Counterintelligence AD. Even though you turned it down, they probably figured it could happen again at any time."

Bursaw said, "I hate to be the bearer of grim reality, but we've still got to prove that Kate is innocent. We can't go to the prosecutor, because Kate is in escaped status, Steve is wanted, and if I show my face, they'll know who the colored guy was. Even if you took this back to the Bureau and got everybody on board, John, wouldn't surveillance and wiretaps take months or longer?"

Vail said, "Luke's right. You're the only one with any mobility, John. Can you go back to your CIA contact and give him what we've found so far and let them run with it?"

"I can, but they're going to do the same surveillance and wiretaps that the Bureau would do. And don't forget it's their agency, so they're not going to be in any hurry to prove that one of their own has gone over. Eventually, because there's no hard evidence, it could get swept under the rug. In the meantime Kate is still wanted."

Vail said, "We have one weapon we're ignoring—the petty jealousies between the Bureau and the CIA. When is Langston due back?"

Kalix said, "He and the director should be returning tomorrow afternoon."

"Go tell your contact that you're repaying him for his information and the photos. Give him everything. But tell him that the director and your boss are due back the day *after* tomorrow, and then you've got to give it to them. Tell him he's got two days to make a move against Rellick if he doesn't want the FBI to make the arrest."

"That just might work. They would do anything to prevent that embarrassment," Kalix said. He unplugged the DVD player and put it in his case. "I'll give you a call as soon as I talk to him."

Bursaw said, "I'll walk you out, John. I want to take a quick stroll around the neighborhood and make sure our friends from the Marshals Service aren't watching us."

After they left, Kate asked Vail, "How'd you see Jennifer and me on that DVD?"

"As good-looking as she is, how do you not see her? To tell the truth, I didn't even notice you."

Kate laughed. "Then how did you know it was Jennifer? You've never met her."

"Like I said, I just saw a pretty girl and wanted to see more of her."

"She's a very good friend, but I've got to tell you, she's very particular about who she dates. White-collar only, so reel it in, bricklayer."

"I'll bet you used to say the same thing."

"Okay, we'll go with 'used to.'"

TWENTY-FOUR

THE PHONE RANG. BURSAW PICKED IT UP AND PUSHED THE Speaker button. "Go ahead, John. We're all here."

"My guy went for it. In two months Rellick is being posted to a foreign assignment. He wouldn't say exactly where, but it sounded like someplace critical. They're about to start a reinvestigation of him, including a polygraph, which is routine with any sensitive assignment. It may be another reason he's still worried about Kate. Anyway, they're going to ambush him with the polygraph first thing tomorrow morning, making some excuse about an upcoming shortage of polygraphers that necessitates it being done now. Once they get him strapped in, it'll be all ahead full on the video and Gulin. That, along with the usual questions about contacts with foreign nationals, accepting money, et cetera, should blow the needles off the box."

"Are you going to be there?"

"Yes. I told him I'd like to watch, just out of curiosity, but I think my pal suspects it's because I want to make sure that they're pushing it. Otherwise we'd have to take over."

"We'll wait to hear from you."

Vail disconnected the line. "Let's hope he breaks."

"And if he doesn't?" Kate asked.

"I'm turning you in for the reward."

"In that case you should take me to dinner tonight. You know, the condemned, a hearty meal and all."

Bursaw said, "There's a couple of decent restaurants within walking distance." They both looked at him as if they'd forgotten he was there. "No, no, I'm not inviting myself."

"Please come, Luke," Vail said with mock insincerity.

He laughed. "Just for that, I should go along. But I have a life of my own to screw up." He got up and slipped on his topcoat. "I'll be by first thing in the morning—unless there's a tie on the doorknob or U.S. Marshals crime-scene tape across the jamb."

DUSK ADDED TO their anonymity as Kate and Vail strolled down M Street, ignoring the falling temperature. She had ahold of his arm and pulled herself closer with each sharp gust of wind. "Sure it's not too cold to walk?" he asked.

"After three days in a cell, it feels good." They were early for their dinner reservation and turned into a brick courtyard that housed several small shops and art galleries to window-gaze. One of them displayed several sculptures and ceramic works. "Anything you like?" she asked idly.

She was wearing Luke's sister's navy camel-hair coat. There was something about the color that made her hair and skin luminous. Her long, dark lashes contrasted her flashing blue eyes perfectly. He took a half step back to look her over. "As a matter of fact . . . there is."

He continued to stare at her until she bumped her hip into his in amused protest. "I was referring to the items on the other side of the glass."

A series of sculptures were displayed, some metal, some bronze and clay. There was even one in wax of a heavy-bodied figure lying on its side in a catatonic curl. A series of semicollapsed ceramic containers caught his attention. They leaned at different angles and, although the same general shape, were different in size. Vail appraised all of them. "These people are legitimate artists."

"I don't get it. Why do you think this stuff is good and yours isn't? I know I've only seen two of your sculptures, but they were at least as good as these."

He waved his hand across the window respectfully. "This isn't about technical ability. There's an instinct involved in creating something like this, an instinct that even they don't understand. They are real artists because they have to let loose on the world what they create. The belief in themselves to say, 'This is my art, and if you don't like it, I don't really care. Here it is anyway. I'd almost rather that you didn't buy it. It's what separates me from people like you.'"

"'People like you'? You actually mean *you*."

"That's right, people like me, because I can't put it out there for anyone to judge."

"Because they might not like it?"

"Everything I do is carefully orchestrated so people aren't allowed to examine me. That's why I sneaked out of that bank robbery, and that's why no one except you has ever seen my sculptures."

"So what you're really saying is that it's not just your art, but you're not willing to put any part of your life out there to examine."

"That's my choice, yes."

"Why would you sculpt if you didn't want anyone to see it?"

"It's something I want to be good at."

"And how will you decide when you're good enough?"

"I guess I'll know."

Kate stared back through the window, carefully measuring what she was about to say. "Now I know why you like being a bricklayer."

"This should be good."

"All brick walls look the same. As long as they're level and straight, they look like every other wall in the world. No creativity, no individuality, and—apparently most important—no judgment."

Vail stared at the objects in the window for a while longer, ignoring the icy wind. Kate stood huddled against him. The expression on his face told her she'd stirred something that had been deeply buried. She waited for one of their arguments to begin.

"On my fourteenth birthday, my father announced to me that he was going to start teaching me to lay brick. I had worked the summers and weekends for years as his laborer, probably since I was ten or eleven. Naturally I was excited to finally learn. I'd watched him for years, envious of his skill. Something a boy does no matter what kind of father he has. That day we were building a chimney, and he let me lay the last three feet of it. When I was done, I thought it looked pretty good, at least for a first try. He sent me down to start cleaning up. Fifteen minutes later he came down without saying a word. The next day I was surprised when we went back to the same job. He put up the ladder and told me to go up on the roof. When I got there, the entire top of the chimney I'd built had been torn down, the bricks scattered all around it. He told me that I'd done a lousy job and that this was the only way I'd learn. He then had me go down and mix the mortar, bring it up, and watch him rebuild it."

"That's awful. But at least you learned how to do it, right?"

Vail laughed with a tinge of anger, not at her but at what he was about to recall. "This wasn't some apprenticeship hazing or poor parenting technique, this was him getting even."

"Even for what?"

"Who knows? For having to raise me by himself. I don't know. It seemed as if his whole life was about getting even with everyone. That's who he was."

"That happened a long time ago."

Vail laughed again, and this time it had an edge to it that told her she was being naïve. "If that had happened once, it would probably be the kind of story you'd laugh at during a Thanksgiving meal, but every time I finished something after that, he would send me to clean up while he stayed behind. I never knew until the next morning whether he'd torn it down or not. Sometimes I wouldn't sleep, wondering if I had pleased my father, which is very important to a fourteen-year-old, especially if there was no one else around. He did it the rest of the summer. If we stopped somewhere for lunch and he started drinking whiskey, I didn't have to wonder—tearing it down would be automatic."

Kate understood now why Vail's approach to work was so intense, why it crowded out everything else. She thought about when she'd recruited him on that Chicago rooftop to help with the Pentad case six months earlier. After she made her appeal, he worked almost in a rage. She thought it was because of what she'd said, but now she wondered if it wasn't because she was invading his privacy, at a time when he held at bay the demons his father had left behind. A feat that became impossible when someone else might be able to detect the tiniest flaw. It had to be why he never stopped working on a case, even after it was *solved*. "Have you ever thought about confronting him and showing him what you've accomplished?"

"Accomplished? I'm a bricklayer."

"Actually, you choose to be a bricklayer. Maybe you continue to do it because it's the only way to show your father how wrong he was. You need to go see him and tell him what you've done, your education, your work with the FBI."

"I can't."

"Why not?"

"I just can't."

"Why not?"

"All right, I won't."

"That's your father. You can't put the rest of your life on hold because of one bad summer."

"You're right, it was only one summer, because by the time I turned fifteen, I could lay brick as well as he could. And, more important, I was much faster, which translated into more money. Not that I ever saw any of it. But when I was sixteen, he found a new way to 'parent.' That entire summer we worked building a hospital, a huge job. There were other contractors on the site—roofers, Sheetrockers, carpenters, everything. I was always big for my age, so he started lining up fights for me. On Fridays he would have me fight grown men for their paychecks. The first time I lost. Three of my ribs were broken. But he was very reassuring. He told me it was all right, because he'd get better odds the next time. Maybe that's why I've never looked forward to paydays. When I turned seventeen, I refused to do it anymore. The next year was—to put it mildly—contentious."

"When's the last time you saw him?"

"My eighteenth birthday. I got up in the morning and packed. He was eating breakfast. I stopped and looked at him. I suppose I wanted him to have some remorse, maybe even try to stop me, but I think he actually looked relieved."

She pulled on Vail's arm to get him to start walking. He took one last look at the pieces in the window. After a few blocks of silence, she said, "Am I really the only one who's seen your sculptures?"

"Even though I told you I didn't want you to look at them, yes."

"Then I'm glad I didn't follow orders. That one of me is—"

"I destroyed it."

"What?"

"A few nights after you left, I sat in front of it, drinking. Finally I got drunk enough to see the truth, so I broke it down."

"What truth? It looked exactly like me."

He stopped and faced her, putting his palm on her cheek. "One of the things I like best about you is that you really don't understand your own beauty. I understand it better than you do, and I don't understand it at all. I had to do that bust of you, to try to understand exactly what it is about you that haunts me. When I destroyed it, I destroyed my obsession with perfection. You're right, me being a bricklayer is about not being judged. But destroying that bust of you was the healthiest thing I've ever done."

Tears started down Kate's face. She buried herself against his chest. "Who are you?"

"Haven't you been listening? For better or worse, I'm a bricklayer." Vail took out a handkerchief and handed it to her. "If it's any consolation, since then—for the first time ever—I've kept the things I've made, all of them. I think I'm actually starting to like what I make."

Kate gave him his handkerchief back and took his arm again. "And will *I* get to see them?"

"You'll have to come to Chicago."

"Uh-oh."

"That's right, Katie, there is an admission price."

They started walking again. "I'm hungry."

"I hope you're speaking biblically."

"I'm talking seafood, Vail, and as much of it as you can afford."

"Well, aren't you the demanding little fugitive?"

"If I were, I wouldn't be dating a bricklayer pretending to be an FBI agent pretending to be a sculptor."

"If I remember my time in the Bureau correctly, everybody was pretending to be an agent."

"That's the problem, no one pretends anymore."

KATE PUT THE key in the lock and turned around to face him, flattening her back against the door. "I had a very nice time tonight, Steven," she said, her voice feigning a this-is-our-first-and-last-date rejection.

She had been relatively quiet during dinner. His flirting usually elicited playful banter from her, but tonight she'd been largely unresponsive, seemingly lost in her own thoughts. He even threw her a couple of lines she could have used to unload on him, but they didn't seem to register. Vail guessed that it was the arrest and the charges pending against her. He knew she was grounded enough to understand that with the evidence they'd uncovered so far, she would never be formally charged and that complete freedom was not far away. But maybe being put in such a precarious position and having to be so dependent on him was causing her to finally understand why he had such disdain for the Bureau. The organization she'd given so much to had been unwilling to risk anything to help her.

But now maybe she was trying to tell him that she'd made some sort of decision. He hoped so.

"I'd like to see you again," he said.

"The truth is, Steven, the last few days I've been spending all my time with women. If you know what I mean."

"If that's supposed to turn me off, you may want to take it in a different direction."

"Let me put it another way—no, we can't see each other again."

"I think I should at least get a good-night handshake."

"Yeah, like that's going to happen."

"Come on, Katherine. How about I come in for a cup of coffee?"

"I don't know, my roommate is a bit of a psychopath." She whispered, "He's in the building trades."

Vail put his hands against the door on either side of her. "Have you two got something going on?" He leaned in and put his cheek against hers.

She nuzzled against the heat of his neck. "It's complicated."

"That sounds like a yes. Is he here now?"

"He's very close by."

He kissed her gently on the mouth. "How close?"

"Very, *very* close."

"I say we chance it."

"Well, that was an expensive dinner," she said.

"I won't stay any more than four or five hours."

"You promise?"

"Certainly no later than spring."

She turned around and opened the door. "Just coffee, right?"

They were inside and quickly dropped their coats where they stood. She threw herself against him and kissed him almost angrily.

He said, "For some reason I have a sudden taste for Girl Scout cookies, too." He unzipped her dress, and she stepped out of it, then unbuttoned his shirt. "You're sure there's no chance of a handshake."

She pulled at the end of his belt. "Absolutely not."

TWENTY-FIVE

THE FIRST GRAY LIGHT OF MORNING SEEPED INTO THE BEDroom, but Vail had been awake for almost a half hour, sitting up, watching Kate sleep. Even the darkness couldn't mask the remarkable balance of her features, which seemed to pulse in the low light. Her hair, though messed by Vail and sleep, had a provocative quality to it. A few strands streaked past her ear, a sheaf above it against the part, rising up and then tracing the contour of her head. More of it fell across her pillow, haloing her perfectly round cheekbones. In a flash he saw his next sculpture: a prone figure, vague, its sex barely discernible until the eye found the hair, displayed exactly like Kate's was now.

As quietly as possible, he got up, taking his pillow. As he reached the bedroom door, he heard her pick up the telephone and, after pretending to dial, say, "Is this 911? Yes, I'd like to report a hit-and-run."

"Luke could be here anytime." He smiled.

She got up and pulled him back into bed. "I don't care if he knows. I don't care if anyone knows."

He threw his pillow next to her. "Actually, I was worried about my reputation."

• • •

VAIL HEARD THE door opening quietly and sat up on the couch. He had moved there just minutes before. The sound of keys jingling against one another on a ring told him it was Bursaw.

Bursaw walked into the living room and looked at Vail's pillow and blanket on the sofa. He shook his head, smiling. "Don't blame me. That restaurant has always worked for me. It'll probably take Kate a while to adjust, what with being locked up with all those good-looking women and you not exactly leading-man material."

"If you think the women in jail are good-looking, it's no wonder that restaurant always works for you."

Bursaw held up a paper bag. "See, that's why I brought you fresh bagels, I know how cranky you get when you haven't eaten in thirty or forty minutes."

Kate came out of the bedroom tying her robe. "Hey, Luke."

"Mmm, mmm, mmm. Now I see why you're the most wanted woman in D.C.—even before you went over the wall."

Kate laughed musically. "Somebody needs coffee awfully bad." She held out her hand for the bag.

"Have you heard anything?" Vail asked him.

"Not a word. I drove by the off-site, and the marshals are still sitting on it."

"Hopefully Kalix is making some progress—otherwise your sister'll have to find a new place to live," Vail said. "I'm going to get cleaned up."

When Vail stepped out of the shower, he could

smell the coffee. And he could hear Kate and Bursaw talking. Occasionally a short burst of her laughter reached him in the bedroom. Unable to make out what they were saying, he sat down on the bed for a while to listen to her laugh.

When he walked into the kitchen, he poured himself a cup of coffee. "You want me to toast a bagel for you, Steve?" she asked.

He tore one in half and said, "Thanks, this is fine."

"So what do you think John's chances are today?"

"I think they're good, but you can't go by me. I'm frequently wrong because of my overly optimistic attitude."

"Actually, you're rarely wrong, precisely because of your cynicism," Bursaw said. "But I got a feeling this *is* turning around."

Kate said, "Is there something else we should be doing? You know, in case John strikes out?"

"I guess I can start going through everything again," Vail said.

She studied his face for a minute. "I don't need you sitting around here reassuring me that everything is all right. If you want something reviewed, I'll do it. You and Luke can make better use of your time looking for Sundra. Besides, watching you sit around here all day will drive me crazy."

"You up for that, Luke?" Vail asked.

"Thanks, Kate. Now I'll have to put up with him all day."

Vail took a last swallow of coffee and said to Kate, "Don't answer the door for anyone. If the phone rings, don't answer it. If you need anything, call Luke's cell."

"Anything specific you want me to look for in the files?"

"Why don't you take a look at all the moles they gave up that lead to you. There's something rattling around in one of the subbasements of my brain telling me we've missed something. There's got to be at least one mistake they made. Maybe something else that'll expose Rellick."

She walked them to the door. "Boys, don't forget to say please and thank you, and absolutely no gunfighting." She pushed them both out the door and locked it.

Once they were in Bursaw's car, Vail said, "Okay, who's next on the deleted-file list?"

"Kate seemed a lot less tense this morning. You wouldn't know anything about that, would you?"

"If you're going to use your Vulcan mind meld, this could turn out to be a very long day."

"Okay, I'll let it drop, but be advised I have made a mental note that there was no denial." Bursaw reached over the seat and grabbed his briefcase. "Let's see." He flipped through some pages. "How about the El Mejor Car Service?"

"Is that Spanish?"

"In this town it could just be misspelled."

The address was in a commercial neighborhood. The building was two stories and ran a long way back into the property. There was parking all around the rear, and several of the cars were older limousines. Vail said, "Let's take a ride through the lot and see if we can figure out what we're looking at here."

Bursaw coasted around the building, which was, judging by the high overhead doors, mostly garage in the back half. Vail looked at the cars that were not part of El Mejor's fleet but more likely belonged to the employees. He pointed out Colombian-flag bumper stickers on two of them. Bursaw said, "You want to pass, maybe come back with some help when you're off the marshals' Top Ten list? I think there's a rule right in the handbook which states that wanted FBI agents should not get into shoot-outs with drug dealers."

"No, I'm feeling very docile today."

Bursaw snorted a single syllable of laughter. "Docile? You? I guess you should 'sleep on the couch' more often." He parked against a back wall near a walk-in door.

As they entered, they counted seven men scattered around five vehicles. The hot smell of oil and grinding metal hung in the warm air. Every one of the workers stopped what he was doing and scrutinized the two agents. No one said anything, and as Vail started to slowly unbutton his topcoat, he and Bursaw casually stepped away from each other, minimizing themselves as targets.

"Who's the boss?" Vail asked. No one answered. "Who's the boss?" he asked again, a little more impatiently.

Still nobody spoke up. He took a couple of steps toward the closest man, who had the dashboard from a Cadillac next to him on a bench and was working on one end of it.

Suddenly, from behind Vail, a man spoke with a slight Hispanic accent. "I am the owner."

Vail turned around as Bursaw continued to watch the men. He flashed his credentials. "We'd like to talk to you."

"Do we have something to talk about?"

"It's not about what you think it is. It's about a missing person. But if you send us on our way, others will come back, and it won't be to talk."

The owner weighed his options. "I guess I have a couple of minutes."

The three men walked into an overly ornate office. "What's your name?" Vail asked.

"Alberto Clark."

"Americanized?"

"My parents did it when we came here. I was three. I didn't know the FBI was so interested in genealogy."

"Actually, we're more interested in true names."

Bursaw handed Clark a photo and said, "Her true name is Sundra Boston."

"And?" Clark asked.

"Know her, seen her, heard of her?"

He handed back the picture. "I don't know her. Why would you think I did?"

"She's an FBI employee, and now she's missing. She was investigating your business."

"This is a legitimate business. I pay taxes. I am a citizen."

"This has been a paid public service announcement," Bursaw said in a sarcastic monotone. "And your employees?"

"I'm not a fool. They are all here legally on work visas."

Vail said, "And those cars out there, the ones they're working on. That's part of your business?"

"Those are their cars. When it's slow, I let them work on them."

Bursaw threw his head back and laughed. "I'd like an employment application because you must have the best wages in America. Those guys don't know three words of English, and they're all driving luxury cars? The one working on the dashboard was swapping VINs. I expected you to lie to me, but try to keep it at a level that's not completely insulting. You're from Colombia. You're supposed to be dealing cocaine, not stolen cars. Have you no ethnic pride?"

"Alberto, we're with the FBI, where lies will get you five years apiece," Vail said. "Now, have you had any contact with the FBI regarding your *business*?"

"No, I swear," Clark answered, the concern growing in his voice.

"Convince us."

Clark thought for a moment. "We've been operating here freely for three years. We have little concern about the police interrupting our operation. Do you think that if we had done something to a federal agent we would be doing business as usual with the door open so any FBI man could walk in?"

Bursaw and Vail looked at each other and shrugged in agreement that it was a strong argument. "We're going to push you—temporarily—to the bottom of our very short list. If we don't come up with something better, we'll be back," Vail said.

"I don't know what else I could do, but if I can help in any way, just call me," Clark said.

As Vail started toward the door, Bursaw said, "I'll be right there."

Five minutes later Bursaw came out of the building and slid in behind the wheel. "What were you doing?" Vail asked. "I'm not going to see you driving a new Cadillac, am I?"

"Actually, I was deputizing my newest informant. We don't really have anybody working stolen cars, so I thought someone with Alberto's talent and range of friends was worth a ninety-day audition. I'm sure he knows other Colombians who still believe in the sanctity of their country's leading export. We do have people working drugs."

Bursaw's cell rang. When he saw that it was Kalix, he handed it to Vail. "No one knows where Rellick is," the deputy assistant director blurted out.

"What happened?" Vail asked.

"Apparently the CIA can be just as inept as the Bureau. One of their polygraphers. They wanted to make sure he'd be available to test Rellick this morning, so they scheduled him yesterday but didn't say anything about this guy possibly being a double agent. Well, you know how examiners are. They have a whole checklist they give the subject the day before. No excessive drinking, no mood-altering drugs, make sure the wind is out of the southeast at no more than eight knots. The people here are theorizing that Rellick might have gotten spooked and took off."

"Are they doing anything to find him?" Vail asked.

"They've called his home, and there's no answer. They're getting a search warrant for his house and bank records. They still don't want us involved in it officially, so they're moving at warp speed before the director and Langston come back."

"Okay, I'm going to let Kate know."

"I'll stay with them until we get an answer one way or the other. Keep your fingers crossed."

TWENTY-SIX

BURSAW PARKED THE BUREAU CAR IN HIS SISTER'S GUEST parking space, and they went up to the apartment. Vail used a key to open the door and yelled inside, "Kate, it's us!"

She came around the corner wearing an apron, a curious expression on her face. "I thought you'd be longer." Then she read something positive in Vail's expression. "You found Sundra?"

"No, not yet." He told her about Rellick's vanishing act. "When John called to tell me, he said the CIA was getting search warrants for his bank and house. There's a good chance that he wouldn't have confessed to the polygrapher, so this might turn out even better."

"Except he had time to clear out anything incriminating."

"You weren't supposed to figure that out, at least not so quickly. Stay positive—this is moving in our favor."

"You're absolutely right," she said. "Lunch is not going to be ready for a while. You guys want something to drink?" she asked with surprising nonchalance.

"No thanks," Bursaw said.

"I'm all set," Vail said. "You're taking this well."

In a faked whisper, she said, "Don't tell anyone, but I've got a couple of really good guys looking out for me."

Bursaw said, "You went and got somebody else?"

After lunch Vail picked up one of the Calculus folders and started rereading it. Ten minutes later he tossed it onto the table in front of him. "That's it, I can't read anymore. I've been over this stuff so much that I wouldn't recognize the answer if it were highlighted."

Bursaw's phone rang; it was Kalix again. He put it on speaker. "I'm with the group going to Rellick's house with a search warrant. They pinged his cell phone, and it shows he's home. I'll call you—we're just about to make entry."

Everyone tried to appear unexcited, as though too much optimism might jinx the outcome. Kate went back to the kitchen, and Bursaw turned on the news. For the next half hour, he listened to the local broadcast. Vail became lost in his thoughts, reexamining everything, looking for another way to prove Kate's innocence in case Rellick proved to be unco-operative. When nothing came to him, he got up and went into the kitchen. He stepped up behind her and slowly pulled on one of the apron strings. "I think I know what we need."

She let him get it completely untied before she turned around. Reaching behind her, she retied it. "Yes, Steve, that's exactly what we don't need right now."

"I never even got a real New Year's kiss." He put an arm around her waist.

"I kissed you. Which, by the way, triggered my one New Year's resolution—to only kiss men in tuxedos."

"I've been thinking about canceling my diving trip and going to maître d' school."

"You greeting people for tips. That sounds like a shorter career than you had with the FBI."

Bursaw's phone rang again. He called in to Vail that it was Kalix. Vail put Kate at arm's length— "It's so easy to mock someone else's dreams"—then walked into the living room and took the phone. "Yes, John."

"Is everyone there?" Kalix asked.

Vail called Kate in from the kitchen and pushed the Speaker button. "We're all here."

"Rellick's gone. He left his phone here and turned it on as a decoy. That's the bad news. But up in his attic, there have to be fifty of those banker's boxes—you know, for storing records. Not only his own, but all kinds of family stuff his parents must have accumulated for decades. Everything—his divorce records, stocks sold twenty years ago. So far they've found five or six of them with classified documents in them, all copies he evidently made. So now the CIA will be able to reconstruct exactly what information he turned over to the Russians. They're most appreciative."

"Will that be enough to clear Kate?"

"It will be with what they found in one of them. Remember on that thumb drive, the typed list of eight FBI-CIA joint investigations along with their named targets? The one that Kate's latent was supposed to have been on?"

Vail looked at Kate. "It was in there?"

"They're going to examine it for prints to see if Rellick's are on it. It hasn't been processed before, so the Russians must have copied it and fumed the copy for the flash-drive setup."

"You'd think Rellick would have destroyed everything, especially that."

"He probably panicked, and maybe he intends to defect. If so, why bother? Considering where this box was, under all the rest, he may have just forgotten it, and even if he didn't, it would have taken him some time to find it in all that mess. From the other documents in the box, it looks like it's a couple of years old, so if he did think about getting rid of it, he probably knew that it would take too long to find."

Vail said, "That sounds like all good news to me."

"For us, yes, but for them there's a new problem. As soon as they discovered he was gone, they unleashed the techs on his work computer. They found a deleted file that he'd cobbled together from a bunch of different files that he shouldn't have been able to gain access to. They're thinking maybe the Russians helped him 'jailbreak' some of the CIA security measures."

"What was on it?" Vail asked.

"Dozens of the agency's European sources. If he's taking it to the Russians, the likelihood of their being killed is quite high. It would set the Agency back ten years."

"You said 'if he's taking it to the Russians.'"

"The last entry in the file was just two days ago. And it was deleted last night after the polygrapher told him about the impending test. So they don't think he had completed the list yet. But somehow they were able to tell that it was downloaded before it was deleted."

"Did they check his e-mail?" Vail asked.

"Both at the office and here. He didn't send it through either of them. I don't know, maybe he put it onto another thumb drive. As you can imagine, there's a fairly large amount of panic around here. Right now they're trying all their super-secret spy stuff to find him. The problem is that he knows how to avoid it," Kalix said. "Steve, they found one more thing on his computer here. That photo that was sent to the two guys at the house who tried to kill you, through that untraceable CIA phone line—it was on there. The Russians must have had him send it so it wouldn't come back to anyone."

"Well, that answers who," Vail said.

"Anyway, before Kate's innocence gets lost in all the impending catastrophe, I'm going to go see the United States Attorney. He says he'll see me as soon as I get there. In the meantime, maybe we can find something else here that will eliminate any doubt that Kate wasn't part of this."

"I don't know how to thank you, John," she said.

"You're not clear yet, Kate. As long as Rellick's on the loose, they are going to need somebody to blame. They've got evidence against you, and even though it's all manufactured, the United States Attorney probably isn't going to be a fan of yours the way you made a fool out of him when you escaped. But I'll let you know once I talk to him."

After Kalix hung up, Vail said, more to himself than the others, "He's right."

"Think so?" Bursaw said.

Realizing he'd said it out loud, Vail looked at Kate. "Sorry. It would be better for you if they found Rellick. Much better."

She thought for a second and then said, "See if this sounds right: Rellick left his cell phone behind at his house, mostly as a decoy. Would he have another one? You know, just for spy business?"

"That makes a lot of sense," Vail said.

"You have that CIA dead-end number, right?"

"Yes."

"Since you were last in the Bureau, we've developed fairly sophisticated reverse-toll record traces, especially for cell phones, because every call is noted for billing. So we can take a call if we know the date and time and, with a fairly simple computer run, determine the phone it was made from."

Vail said, "So if Rellick does have another cell and we can identify it through the reverse records, if he's got it on, we can ping it."

"And find out where he is," Bursaw added.

Vail had his pocket notebook out, turning pages. "Here it is." He started to write it down, then stopped. "But how do we get it done? Technically, you're still wanted."

"If you think about it, there aren't many people at headquarters who know my situation. The worst thing that could happen is that someone could find out I'm here. We really have no choice." Both men nodded. "Why don't you guys get out of here, and I'll make the call. That way if something happens to me, you'll still be able to look for Rellick."

"Just remember, if you get locked up again, you're on your own."

"Talk about your one-night stands."

Vail looked over at Bursaw, who had a huge, self-congratulatory smile on his face. "Thanks, Kate. Now I can spend the rest of the day fending off questions from the Special Agent Lust here."

AFTER EATING BURGERS in the car again, Vail and Bursaw sat parked a half mile from the apartment, where Kate was making calls. "Steve, do you think we'll actually find out what happened to Sundra?"

"Huh? Oh, I don't know. We could. Right now I'd guess fifty-fifty."

"You're worried about Kate, aren't you?"

Vail looked at him carefully to make sure this wasn't a lead-in to a salacious line of questioning. "The way everything's gone today, I shouldn't be, but every once in a while I get worried that things won't work out. That usually happens when I can't do anything except sit and wait." He took Bursaw's phone and dialed Kate. After a number of rings, he hung up. "Does your sister have call-waiting?"

"I think so."

"I didn't get the machine, so hopefully Kate was busy on the line."

Then almost immediately the phone rang, and Vail could see that it was Kate. "Everything okay?" he asked.

"Put me on speaker. . . . It looks like we got Rellick's second cell. They queried that CIA dead-end number on the date and time you gave me and came up with a phone whose subscriber is William Jackson, with a billing address at that Russian safe house in Denton you tried to burn down. There were a number of calls on it from another cell that comes back to a Vladimir Demeter, same billing address. I'm sure they're both aliases, one for Rellick and the other is probably Calculus's, since the two of them were meeting regularly around that time."

"And you're having them ping Rellick's number?" Vail asked.

"They've already started, but it's not on right now. They'll ping it every ten minutes. Our people at headquarters are going to track it with the Bureau satellite. Where are you?"

"About a half mile from you."

They heard her other line click in. "Okay, hold on."

Bursaw said, "You ever think about moving here?"

"You mean because of Kate?"

"We've got brick buildings, too."

"I'm thinking Kate's a little too well adjusted to handle me full-time."

"Hey, contrarians need love, too."

"That's true, they do, but never each other."

"In philosophy that would constitute a paradox. Just remember, a paradox, while seemingly illogical, is in fact true."

"Go ahead, caller, you're on the line with the love doctor."

"Deflection is a sure sign of hitting a nerve."

"Yeah, the auditory nerve."

They heard Kate click back. "They've got him.

He's not far away. The GW Memorial, heading north just below the Arlington Memorial Bridge."

Bursaw put the car in gear. "We're on our way."

It was starting to grow dark, and the evening traffic was getting heavier. Just as Bursaw's car reached the on-ramp for the GW Memorial Parkway, his phone rang again. Kate said, "He's pulled off the GW just after the Roosevelt Bridge. The only thing there is the parking area for Roosevelt Park."

Vail said, "I told you the Russians love parks. He may be meeting his handler there. If so, they're probably going to try to get him out."

"I'll have them keep tracking him in case he starts moving. I'll call you back in five."

Bursaw pulled into the lot. There was only one car, a midsize Chevrolet. It was freshly washed, and there was a car-rental sticker on its bumper. Both men drew their guns and, leaving their doors open should they need cover to retreat to, approached the car from opposite sides. It was empty.

Bursaw said, "He must have crossed the footbridge into the park. There's nowhere else to go."

"Is there another way out of there?"

"It's an island. The footbridge is the only way on or off, unless you want to swim across a freezing Potomac."

"How many flashlights do you have?"

"Just one."

"Okay, you lock up the car and I'll make sure he can't drive out of here."

As Bursaw went to the trunk to get the light, he watched Vail pull out his lockback knife and slash all four tires of the rental. Then he took out his phone and turned it on. "Put yours on vibrate," he told Bursaw. "We're going to have to split up. When we get across the bridge, you go north and I'll take south. If you spot him, call me and we can pin him in."

Vail then called Kate. "I've turned my phone on. It looks like Rellick's in the park. Luke and I are going to split up. Just keep on Rellick's phone." He hung up. "Ready?" he asked Bursaw.

"I don't think we should cross the bridge together. If he's waiting for us, all he'll have to do to take both of us out is fire straight along the bridge. There's no place to get cover unless we're willing to go into the water."

"Sounds right. You go first."

"Hey, it's your girlfriend we're trying to get off."

Vail stepped onto the footbridge. "Okay, but next New Year's I'm definitely getting a hooker. In Chicago."

TWENTY-SEVEN

AS SOON AS VAIL REACHED THE OTHER SIDE, HE TOOK UP A defensive position to cover Bursaw while he crossed the bridge. He checked his watch—almost eight o'clock. It was dark, but there was enough light from the roadways crisscrossing the island to follow the footpaths. Without a word the two men glanced at each other, Vail heading south and Bursaw north.

Vail walked a hundred feet and then stopped to listen. Since the only car in the lot besides Bursaw's was the rental, Vail felt that Rellick had to be there waiting for someone to arrive. Possibly one of the Russians, so he could exchange the list he'd downloaded from the CIA files for a way out of the country and probably one last, very large payment. Rellick still had his phone on, so there was a good chance he was making calls or waiting for one. A gust of frigid wind came off the Potomac, and Vail waited for it to subside before he continued.

He was surprised at how rustic the park was. Except for the footpaths, some of which were endless three-foot-wide wooden planks, the ground was heavy with trees and undergrowth, creating more of a wooded setting than an urban park. There were very few evergreens, and the hardwoods were bare.

The path he was on was dirt, and there were still leaves cluttering it. The lights from the surrounding cities allowed him to find his way south.

Off to his left, Vail could see a frozen pond. He took out his phone and made sure it was on. As he neared the southern end of the island, he could see the tall buildings of Arlington across the Potomac. There was another path off to the right, and it seemed to head toward the great dark shadow of the Theodore Roosevelt Memorial Bridge as it passed overhead connecting D.C. to Arlington.

He thought he heard something and stopped. After thirty seconds the wind blew from the same direction where the suspected sound originated, and this time he recognized an indistinguishable voice. Vail thumbed the safety off his Glock and lightened his step, moving toward its source.

It seemed to be coming from the bridge's underpass, a corridor of fifteen-foot-high off-white concrete walls that curved overhead. At the other end, Vail could see the lights of downtown Arlington reflected off the Potomac. He stopped again and listened. Now, because of the hum of the tires driving over the bridge, he seemed to be in some acoustical dead space, because the voice suddenly vanished. It was the perfect place for spies to meet on a winter night. Especially for Russians, who loved parks, the cold, and vodka.

At the midpoint of each of the walls were walk-in doors, probably leading to maintenance storage. Vail wondered if Rellick had somehow gotten into one of them to wait. He started toward the closest one with his weapon pointed at the other.

When he reached the door, he tried the knob. It was locked.

All of a sudden, ahead of him, around the end of the concrete wall, he heard a man's voice. "Call me back in five minutes, Tanner. . . . I'm not going to wait much longer. . . . Where else would I be?" Rellick walked around the corner and into view as he ended the call. Vail pointed the automatic at him. "That's it, Rellick, FBI. Right there."

The CIA agent raised his hands, still holding the phone. Glancing up at the lighted screen, Rellick pushed a couple of buttons and placed his finger on another, ready to press it. "Unless you want that list of European informants to be e-mailed to the Russian embassy, you'd better drop the gun." He lowered his hands slowly but confidently.

"How do I know you've actually got it on your phone?" Vail asked.

"By now you know I've downloaded the list. And I would need a quick way to send it from anywhere, even here, if I got in a tight spot. So I put it on speed dial. I thought it would be better than a gun. Was I wrong?"

Vail knew by Rellick's confidence that the list had to be on the phone. He dropped his gun on the ground. As soon as he did, Rellick drew a small revolver. "Now walk over here."

Suddenly Vail felt his cell phone vibrate. It was probably Kate, ready to tell him that Rellick and his cell phone were under the bridge. Vail kept walking slowly, hoping to get close enough to make some kind of move. But when he was five feet away, Rellick said, "That's close enough, on your knees. And put your hands in your pockets." Vail did as he was told and wrapped his hand around his knife. But he knew that even if he could get it out in time and open it, Rellick would still be too far away. Rellick carefully cleared the screen on his phone and put it in his overcoat pocket.

"Meeting your handler here?" Vail asked.

"My handler?" Rellick burst out laughing. "My handler offered to get me to Moscow, where I'd be a hero. I'd rather live in a federal prison than in Russia. So I told him I wanted a million dollars for the list. With that much money, I can live fairly comfortably in South America."

"So he says he's bringing you a million dollars here? Tonight?"

"You sound skeptical."

"The banks are closed, and I seriously doubt they keep that kind of cash at the embassy. I hope you didn't tell him where the list was." Rellick didn't answer. "You did. Myles, I think Moscow and federal prison aren't your only options. I'd consider the possibility of death. And not in that order."

"Shut up," Rellick said. "I've got to get out of here. That leaves only one option for you, and it isn't Moscow or federal prison. Unless you can come up with a fourth option." He raised his revolver. "No. Then death it is." Vail took his hands halfway out of his pockets and got ready to charge him; he had nothing to lose.

A gun exploded, and it took an instant for Vail to realize that the shot had come from behind him. The CIA agent looked surprised, even indignant, that a bullet had wound up piercing his chest instead of Vail's. Suddenly the hand holding his gun went limp, and the weapon dropped to the ground. He looked past Vail and tilted his head in confusion at the black man moving quickly toward him, ready to fire a second shot. Then he looked around as if wondering where he was and fell forward heavily, landing on his face. Bursaw snapped on his flashlight and moved past Vail, keeping his gun trained on Rellick in case another shot was needed.

It was then that Vail realized that his vibrating phone call with Rellick's location had gone to Bursaw first.

"Do you think you waited long enough, Luke?"

Bursaw's smile verged on laughter. "Remember that time you left me out in the cold and I got really sick?" He rolled over the body and holstered his weapon.

"Again with that. You know, at a certain point the need for revenge can become very unflattering."

"Not when it's you on your knees."

"I hope we're finally even." Vail took Rellick's cell phone out and made sure it was still on. Then he slipped it into his pocket. "No one needs to know that I've got this."

"Because . . . ?"

"If we give it back to the CIA today, it'll be worth a very nice thank-you. Give it back in a week and it will be . . ."

"Priceless," Bursaw finished.

"Maybe that Ivy League education wasn't wasted." Vail called Kate on his phone. "Rellick's dead."

"Both you guys okay?"

"We're fine."

"Should I ask?"

"Actually, it was Luke who shot him. Can you call Metro Homicide or the Park Police, whoever's jurisdiction this is?"

"Sure. Then I'm coming there."

"I appreciate it, but we're probably not going to be here very long. And you're not out of the woods yet, so let's not push it. When I find out where we're going, I'll let you know."

"You're sure?"

"Call Kalix and fill him in about what's going on." Vail hung up.

Bursaw was searching the body. He pulled out a stack of hundred-dollar bills, held them up for Vail to see, and then stuffed them back in the dead agent's pocket. "He doesn't have ID on him."

Rellick's phone rang. Vail took it out. "Excuse me a minute, I've got to talk to this Russian," Vail said. He pushed the Talk button. "Yeah."

The voice on the other end immediately became suspicious. "What is your name?" Vail knew the caller was asking for Rellick's code name.

"Rumpelstiltskin." The line went dead. Vail put the phone back in his pocket.

"You didn't really think you were going to fool him, did you?"

"I wanted two things: to see if he had a Russian accent, which he did, and for his call to go through, so his number would be in the phone company's computer." Vail checked his watch and noted the time of the call.

• • •

VAIL AND BURSAW explained to the responding Park Police what had taken place on Roosevelt Island so that the crime-scene examination could be conducted. Then they followed a couple of their detectives to their investigative offices in southeast D.C. Once there, the two agents were taken to separate interview rooms. When Vail finished, it was a little after four in the morning. He found Kate waiting in the reception area. "Everything all right?" she asked after hugging him.

"I don't think they handle as many homicides as Metro does, so their process was a little slower."

"What did you tell them?"

"The truth—the other guy did it." And then, without mentioning Rellick's cell phone, Vail explained about how the rogue CIA agent had gotten the drop on him and Bursaw had shot him to save Vail's life.

Just then Bursaw walked out. Kate gave him a hug, too. "They're not keeping you?" she said, an impish grin pulling at the corners of her mouth.

He laughed. "Careful, I could tell them who you really are." They left the building and started walking to the car. Bursaw said, "How about you, what's your status? I see you're out in public without a disguise."

"As soon as I got hold of the Park Police, I called John. He had just met with the United States Attorney. He picked me up at your sister's place and brought me here."

"I hope you're going to tell me we're all off the hook," Bursaw said.

"As far as I know, they never figured out who you were."

"Thank God."

Vail said, "How come you black guys are always complaining about how we all think you look alike until there's a lineup?"

"Kate, did I ever tell you about the dead guy we found wearing a negligee in the doghouse and what Vail had to do to get a confession from his wife?"

Vail waved his hand back and forth. "I don't think that's pre-breakfast conversation."

"I'm begging you, Luke, tell me," Kate said. "What—"

Vail interrupted. "I believe you were about to tell us how we're no longer in fugitive status."

"Okay—for now. To answer your question, Luke, everyone is off the hook. John said he was a little worried when he went to see the United States Attorney. Remember, he played Assistant Director William A. Langston on the phone when he called him to spring me. But I guess he disguised his voice enough that the USA didn't catch on. Anyway, John explained everything we found out about Rellick and his subsequent flight and how he tried to kill an agent. John said he huffed and puffed for a while but then decided that the evidence the CIA had gathered was convincing enough to drop the charges against me."

"And Luke and I?"

"Like I said, they never pulled Luke up on the radar, but you were identified and kind of marked as the ringleader. He said the USA was reluctant to give a pass to a jailbreaker. But then John reminded him that the press would probably view my detention as a serious violation of my rights. And although he might try to mitigate that through some convenient interpretation of national-security protocol, it wouldn't play well because that whole secrecy thing was created to catch the big fish, and since that was supposed to be me, it was no longer an excusable tactic. Finally he told him that I would seek no punitive action against his office if everything were dropped, against everyone. After weighing his liabilities for a few seconds, he agreed. On his way to get me, John called the director and brought him up to speed. He wants all of us in his office at nine A.M."

Kate glanced at Vail, expecting him to offer an excuse as to why he wouldn't be there. "You do know he's probably going to thank you?" she said.

Vail just shrugged his shoulders, making her wonder what he was up to now.

AFTER A PREDAWN breakfast, Bursaw dropped Kate and Vail at his sister's apartment. "Sure I can't give you a ride?"

Kate said, "I want to clean up around here a little. We'll get a cab."

While Kate vacuumed, Vail packed up the files that had been taken from the Sixteenth Street offsite. Then he called a cab and fed the fish while they waited for it to arrive.

Once they were in the taxi, Kate asked, "Why

are you going to the director's meeting? You hate things like that."

"Is that your real question, or do you want to know when I'm leaving?"

"Both, I guess."

"I told Luke I'd help him with his case. That means I'm going to need credentials a little longer. Hopefully the director won't mind giving me a couple of extra days."

"Then off to Florida."

"So far. Would you consider coming along?"

"I might be talked into it."

"Sun, warm water, gallons of rum, and me. The good, the bad, and the ugly. You can claim an alcohol-induced state to excuse the inevitable regrets you'll have afterward."

She smiled absentmindedly. "You know the director is going to offer you the job again."

"I suppose."

"And?"

"I'll listen."

"And then turn him down."

"Kate, we've been through this."

Her eyes softened as she looked away from him. "Do you know what our problem is? Two people cannot get involved with each other, truly involved, without becoming vulnerable, and that is something you and I have guarded against our entire lives." She smiled sadly. "Sorry, I was just hoping—you know. But no one understands better than Steve Vail how frivolous hope is."

"Hope isn't necessarily frivolous, but by inference it is a long shot," he said. "Right now you're still unsettled with all of this. Anybody would be. You may think you want things to be a little more permanent, but give it a couple of days. You go back to work, put up with me hanging around for a while, and then we'll figure out where everything is going."

She looked directly at him again and steadied her eyes against his gaze. "Right now I am feeling vulnerable, and for the first time in my life I'm not afraid of it. Maybe because I know that no matter what happens, you'll be there. That's a nice feeling."

"I'm happy for you, Kate. I genuinely am. I don't know if that's a possibility for me." He turned and watched out the window. She realized he was struggling to understand that kind of commitment.

"So, Vail," she said, her voice now lightheartedly official in an effort to change the mood, "I'm curious. Are you satisfied that we got everybody? You seem distracted since John gave us the news."

Vail turned back and gave her a small, courteous smile. "You know I'm never satisfied. I'm afraid that tomorrow I'll find that chimney torn down again."

"I know when you start thinking that way, there usually is someone else involved."

"Does anything bother you about this case?"

"Do you mean other than me being thrown in prison?"

Vail laughed. "Yes, other than that."

"We've talked about this before. Why did they kill all the double agents?"

"And our best guess was that they didn't want

to embarrass Moscow with revelations of Russia spying against the U.S. But then why didn't they kill Rellick? He said they wanted to take him to Moscow because he had been exposed."

"Did they?" she asked. "Maybe they were setting him up to kill him, too. They just didn't know where he was."

Vail thought about the list of CIA informants Rellick was trying to sell and conceded that maybe Kate was right, that they would have killed him once they had the information. "You're probably right."

"What difference does it make? All those who should go to hell are on their way. And you and I are talking about scuba diving."

"We'll see."

"I really hope you're talking about the scuba diving."

WHEN THE CAB pulled up to Kate's apartment, she said, "Do you want to come in?" She knew he wouldn't, because she could see he was still distracted. And she suspected that her talk about vulnerability was making him cautious.

"Thanks, Kate, but I've got some things I need to do."

"Well, that's certainly vague enough," she said. "Tell me the truth, what are the chances of my seeing you at the director's office tomorrow morning?"

"I don't think I really belong there. You guys will be celebrating, and after Florida I'll be back in Chicago scratching for work."

"Did it ever occur to you that maybe the director

would feel better about your turning him down if he could thank you in person?"

"He asked me to work on a case, not his feelings."

"I hope you're not planning on sneaking out of town tonight."

"I told you, I'm going to help Luke for a couple of days—or at least until we run out the rest of those leads," Vail said. "Why would you think I would do that? I came here to see you."

"And you've seen me. All of me."

"Let me just say in my defense, dating a jailbird isn't all that easy."

She leaned over and kissed him lightly on the lips. "We prefer 'ex-con.'"

TWENTY-EIGHT

KATE WAS THE LAST TO ARRIVE AT THE DIRECTOR'S OFFICE. "Good morning," Bob Lasker said. "It looks like everyone is still standing. Nice work, people." Nodding at Kate, he said, "I thought Steve might be coming with you."

"I think he didn't want to turn down another of your job offers. And you know how he likes to be thanked."

"He hasn't gone back to Chicago already, has he?"

"He promised me he wouldn't, but . . ." She shrugged her shoulders.

"I can't figure out what drives him."

"I'm sure hearing that would make him very happy, sir."

The director laughed. "Okay, let's get down to business." He turned to Bursaw. "Luke, let's start with you. Do you have any aspirations to come to headquarters?"

"Me? Coming to this building every day? I'm sorry, sir, but I enjoy bad-mouthing management far too much to give it up."

"I guess that answers the question of why Steve

trusts you. Just remember you have a Get Out of Jail Free card should you need one."

"I'm sure you won't have to hold on to it for very long."

"And, Kate, you'll go back to your old job as deputy AD simply because of the amount of paperwork that has piled up in your absence. I wouldn't give that to my worst enemy."

"Nothing would make me happier."

"So do we have any loose ends we need to tend to?" No one said anything. "No. Then I've got one more item of interest. Bill Langston has been reassigned as AD in charge of training at Quantico. Effective immediately, I am appointing John Kalix to the position of assistant director of counterintelligence. I'm concerned about how the Russians manipulated the Bureau and almost destroyed the reputation of a deputy assistant director. John was involved, sometimes to the point of great personal danger, in the entire investigation and because of that is more equipped, I feel, to prevent it from happening again."

Kalix's face was expressionless. Apparently the director had told him of the promotion previously. Kate recalled Kalix's comment that Langston had ordered an end to the investigation into whom the Russian handler Gulin had met with at the antique mall. If it had been pursued more thoroughly, Rellick probably would not have been able to do so much intelligence damage, and there would have been no need to frame Kate. She smiled. "Congratulations, John." But she couldn't help wondering if Kalix had been the one to tell the director about Langston's misstep. She decided it didn't really matter. He had helped her escape custody, cleared her through his contacts, and actually saved Vail's life in the process. Even if he had dimed out his boss, she had to give him a pass.

"Okay," the director said, "everybody get out of here and go back to work."

KATE OPENED THE door to her office. The piles of mail and reports completely covered her desk. She stepped around behind it and started prioritizing the stacks. After an hour she could see that it was going to take at least a week of twelve- to fourteen-hour days to catch up. But suddenly there seemed to be a greater priority—to find out what Vail was doing. She locked the door and headed for the garage.

She let herself into the Sixteenth Street off-site and found Vail lying on the couch staring up at the wall. There seemed to be even more paper covering it than she remembered. Vail looked over at her absentmindedly and then back at the wall without saying anything. He hadn't shaved and appeared to not have slept. "I thought you might be sleeping," she said.

"I found a spy we missed."

"What?"

Vail got up. "I'm starving. Do you want something?" He went into the kitchen and took some cold cuts out of the refrigerator for a sandwich.

"No." She followed him. "Who did we miss?"

Without answering her, he started to make the

sandwich, and although he wouldn't look at her, she could see a small smirk on his face. She slapped his arm. "Come on, Vail."

He put the sandwich on a paper plate and walked into the workroom. On the table was a digital recorder. He pushed the Play button and took a bite of his sandwich.

"Hello, it's me—you know, Preston. I've got those infrared facial-recognition schematics you wanted, but the price has gone up. This time I want a hundred thousand dollars in cash, just for me. I've been getting the short end while taking all the chances. So this will keep it, you know, level and true. You've got my number."

"Notice anything about that?" Vail asked. There was a knock downstairs. Kate didn't answer, so he pressed Play again. "I'll get the door."

It was Bursaw. "Next time you're going to skip a meeting, how about letting me know? I don't enjoy being that close to the director."

"He's an honorable man."

"He's still *the* boss. My personnel file has many unanswered questions in it that I don't need someone at that level looking at."

"Come on, Kate's upstairs."

When they walked into the workroom, Kate was a little animated and said, "I think I know what you're talking about, Steve. Hi, Luke."

Vail said to her, "Okay, fire away."

Vail looked at Bursaw to see if he was curious. "Do I need to know?" he asked.

"It's part of the Russian business. It's something I'm going to have to take care of before we get back to Sundra."

"I thought everyone was dead."

"Apparently we missed one," Vail said.

"And I assume, because I'm going to be given the SS blood oath again, that no one else is to know about whatever the new plot calls for."

Kate said, "Don't you think we owe it to John Kalix to cut him in on this? He's an AD now." Kate told Vail about the promotion that morning.

"Then we owe it to him to keep him out of it. He's back to the rules. Let's allow him to enjoy his promotion for a day or two before we make him sorry he accepted it. Luke, can you give us a hand?"

Bursaw shook his head. "Okay, but this time I want first shot at the insanity plea."

Although Vail had given Bursaw the broad strokes of the Calculus investigation when he'd agreed to help with Kate, he hadn't told him the specifics about how the double agents had been un-covered through the Ariadne thread left by the Rus-sians. "The first clue was a series of dots and dashes etched into the side of the DVD that Calculus left for us. That led us to a phone in the Russian em-bassy and an access code. Here's the message." He played it again for Bursaw.

Then Vail said, "And now, since the deputy as-sistant director has apparently figured out where we went wrong, she'll explain."

She said, "Let me give you a brief rundown on how we found these moles. The first one, Charles Pollock, we were given his initials and, to simplify it, where he worked. From that we recovered a DVD that recorded him trading classified documents for cash. In each case that's what we were supplied with, a way to identify the mole and physical evidence of his spying. And in each case there was a hidden or coded clue about how to find the next one. These are what we followed that led to recovering the phony evidence against me. Are you with me so far?"

"Yes."

"So on the Pollock DVD, besides the payoff, the edge had, in Morse code, a telephone number. When we called the number, we got that message you just heard played. And, as you heard at the end of it, there was a touch-tone number being dialed. We assumed that it was another code to identify the caller named Preston who was talking about the infrared technology at the beginning of the recording. We broke down that code, and it led up to a bank box that belonged to Yanko Petriv, the NSA translator. Things were moving pretty fast right then, so we went after Petriv, thinking he was the one selling the facial-recognition schematics. But what we didn't take the time to consider was that Petriv was born in Bulgaria and would probably have an accent, since he spoke Eastern European languages well enough to be a translator. The voice on the recording is definitely American, maybe upper Wisconsin or Minnesota. And he's talking about some very classified technology. Not something a translator would have access to."

Bursaw said, "Let me see if I got this right. The Preston recording is not this guy Petriv, but someone working in technology, selling it to the Russians."

"Right."

"That means that the recording is the evidence?"

"It's not as prominent as the others, but that's what it looks like. That's part of the reason we skimmed over it and missed him."

"So how are you supposed to identify him?"

"I don't know. The whole thing was a sham so I'd wind up in prison and out of Rellick's way. It didn't have to be flawless. It just had to move us along the chain of spies until it got to me."

Vail said, "For it to be convincing, there had to be enough information contained in the phone message for us to identify him. That's the only possibility."

"Play it again, Steve," Bursaw said.

Vail started the recorder and set it down on the table between them. When it finished, Bursaw smiled. "Did you hear it?"

"Hear what?" Vail asked.

"'Level and true.' Did you notice how it's emphasized slightly? Just like 'Preston.'"

Vail played it again, and he and Kate listened more closely. "You're right," he said.

Bursaw went over to the desktop computer and queried "level and true."

"'The Air Force Song,'" he said. "Fourth verse, second line: 'Keep the wings level and true.'"

"Our guy is in the air force," Vail said. "That makes a lot more sense with the 'infrared facial-recognition schematics.' And who knows what else he has access to and is selling to the Russians right now? Someone with this kind of access could do a ton of damage."

Kate said, "There's a lot of air force personnel within a hundred miles."

"Not with access to classified documents about cutting-edge technology," Vail added.

"The Pentagon," Bursaw said.

"That's where I'd start."

"But why did they make it so hard to recognize the clue?" Kate asked.

"They were all hard to recognize. Remember how long the code on the edge of the DVD took, how we thought it was a dead end. This one was just a little too hard, a little too easy to step over. We were looking for codes. This one was audio. They probably figured better too hard than too easy. Too easy might have tipped us off. And if we did miss one, the next clue was provided. Which is what happened."

"Okay," Bursaw said, "what do we do now? There's got to be twenty thousand people working at the Pentagon. It's not like we can just walk in and start demanding answers."

"You're right, Luke, but there is someone who can," Kate said.

"Who?" the two men asked at the same time.

"Tim Mallon."

"The Reston PD chief?" Vail asked.

"I told you he worked nothing but applicant and security clearance cases for twenty-five years. He knows more people at the Pentagon than anyone in the Bureau. And I believe he owes you a favor or two."

"Can you call him?"

Kate picked up the phone and dialed information.

While she was talking to Mallon, Vail said to Bursaw, "Have you had a chance to do any checking on the last two of Sundra's files?"

"Actually, I've been going over her phone records again. Seeing if they matched anything we've run into yet." Bursaw glanced over at Kate, who was still on the phone. "Not to change the subject, but I don't suppose there's any chance of you accepting the director's offer."

"Why?"

"Purely selfish reasons. Maybe it's the philosopher in me, but I too like chaos."

"I'm afraid it would create more problems than it would solve."

"The worst thing that could happen is you'd get fired or quit. That's hardly virgin territory for you."

"Walking away doesn't end all problems."

"Is it Kate?"

"She is certainly part of the geometry."

"Maybe if you were around here permanently, your problems would solve themselves."

Vail laughed. "A man so understanding of the complexities of the fairer sex, how come you never got married?"

"Steve, you've just asked a question that contains its own answer."

Kate finished her call. "Your luck's holding, bricklayer. Tim's downtown at a lunch meeting. He's going to stop by in a half hour."

"I'll get cleaned up."

When Vail reappeared freshly shaved and showered, Kate was introducing Tim Mallon to Bursaw. The two men shook hands, and then Mallon made

his way over to Vail, offering his hand. "Steve, how
are you?"

"I'm good. I haven't been shot since New Year's.
How are those two boys?"

"The Walton boy is fine. Hardly broke stride.
And Eddie Stanton is getting along with his parents.
He's seeing a therapist, too. They're very optimistic."

"I'm glad. Has Kate briefed you about what we
need?"

"Just what she told me on the phone. That you
needed to make a few, very discreet contacts at the
Pentagon, specifically with the air force."

"Tim, I'm going to tell you only the minimum
you need to know. Not because you're no longer
with the Bureau, but because we're not telling
anyone else in the FBI about this, not even the director. I hope you won't feel slighted."

"I'm a little embarrassed to say I'm still eating
free lunches off what you did. I don't think it's possible for me to feel anything but gratitude."

Vail told him that they were working a counterintelligence matter and then played the Preston tape for him. "We believe that this man is a
member of the air force working at the Pentagon.
We need to identify him without him getting wind
of it. We're hoping you'll be able to narrow it down
by the information he mentioned on the tape. That
technology has to be singular in nature. Of course,
the fewer people at the Pentagon that you have to
tell, the better."

"Will I be able to play them the tape?"

"Yes, but again, the more people who hear it, the
harder it'll be to keep this under wraps."

"Steve, I'll do whatever you and Kate want, but I don't know if I have a feel for all these nuances—who to tell, who to let listen. I can get to the right people, but who's told what is a tough call."

"I guess you're right. Will it be a problem if Kate goes with you?"

"More of an asset, if you know what I mean."

"Kate, do you see any problem going with him?"

"You don't want to go?"

"People might not notice two FBI agents, but three could start speculation. Besides, I've got some things I have to get done with Luke."

She took the digital recorder and put it in her purse. "I guess Tim and I can handle it. But before I go, I wanted to show you something in the kitchen."

Vail followed her from the room, and when they were out of sight, she pushed him back against the refrigerator, pinning him with her body. "Allowing little Kate to run a lap all by herself. You'd better be careful, someone might think you're letting your guard down."

He put his arms around her and said, "We've been too busy to get you drunk, so I had to try something."

She gave him a quick kiss on the lips. "Well, Silky, it just might be working." She pushed off him and headed toward the living room.

He called after her. "Said the good-looking blonde as she headed for the safety of witnesses."

TWENTY-NINE

IT WAS DARK WHEN KATE GOT BACK FROM THE PENTAGON. Bursaw had taken off to WFO to put in an "end of the day" appearance for his supervisor. Vail could hear Kate's footsteps coming up the marble staircase. She rushed into the room. "I think we found him," she called out as soon as she saw him.

"Where's Tim?"

"He said he had a meeting with the town council that he couldn't miss. Actually, I think he was trying to impress you with his modesty by not bringing the news himself."

Vail looked at her patiently, tipping his head to one side, telling her not to draw it out herself.

"Okay, okay," she said, "the air force guy. I'm getting to that. Who knew that working applicants for decades would have an upside? Tim seemed to know everybody. The first stop was this air force colonel. He was in charge of personnel there. Tim explained about the sensitivity of the inquiry, and this guy was great. He explained that whatever he gave us would have to go through his commanding officer, who is an air force general. So I made the decision—let's go see him right now. He told the colonel to let us have carte blanche. The only thing he wanted was to be given the heads-up should we have to arrest one of his people. I told him I'd personally call him. The colonel found the infrared facial-recognition drone project almost immediately. We played the tape for him, and he didn't recognize the voice. He determined there were eight individuals assigned to it who could have had access to the actual plans. One is a woman, so she's out. Of the remaining seven, four are still there. The others either have finished their hitch or were transferred. Now it gets interesting. One of them disappeared over a year ago. They're still carrying him as AWOL, an E-5 staff sergeant named Richard David Gallagher. I got a copy of his service record. The colonel also gave me copies of the other six."

She handed Gallagher's file to Vail, and he flipped through its pages until he found what he was looking for. "Did you read this?"

"I haven't had a chance."

He handed it back to her. "Let me see the rest of them while you take a look."

She read a few pages and closed the file. Vail looked at her, and she said, "He was born and raised in Texas. Whatever accent Preston has, it's not Texan. I thought with him taking off, I was onto something, because we don't know how old that recording is."

"Actually, I think you are. The percentage of air force E-5s going AWOL has to be about zero. He may not be Preston, but that he's missing may not be a coincidence." Vail went back to reading the other files. When he looked at the fourth one, he read the first page and then handed it to Kate. He went over to the computer and started typing.

"Master Sergeant Chester Alvin Longmeadow, E-7, grew up in Patzau, Wisconsin."

Vail punched one last key on the computer and, watching the screen, said, "Which is in northern Wisconsin on the Minnesota border."

"He's had several Article Fifteens, whatever that is, for drinking-related incidents," Kate said, continuing to read the file.

"They're administrative actions taken by his commanding officers when something isn't court-martial serious. And it's not unusual for a double agent to have a drinking problem, or a gambling problem, or women problems. Actually, I believe it's a requirement."

"So do you think this is him?" Kate asked.

When Vail didn't answer, she looked over at him. He got up and started exploring the information on the wall. "Longmeadow—that's an unusual name. I've seen it before." He looked at the reports and files scattered around the room. To himself he said, "Please tell me I don't have to go through all this again."

He went to the window and pulled up the shade. Sitting down, he let his stare reach the old Russian embassy across the street. He picked up a pencil and tapped its eraser on the tabletop like a drumstick. Finally Vail snapped to his feet and walked over to a smaller table, where Bursaw had piled up the printouts from Sundra's laptop. He took them and sat down on the couch. "Can you call Luke and run Longmeadow's name by him?"

"You think he's involved in the analyst's disappearance? That doesn't make any sense."

"I know. For some reason I've got it in the back of my mind it's connected. Maybe Luke can eliminate it."

Kate dialed Bursaw's cell. "Luke, it's Kate. We got some names at the Pentagon that could be Preston. Steve wants me to run one by you—Chester Alvin Longmeadow. He thinks it might have come up in Sundra's case." She listened a moment and then said to Vail, "He's not sure."

"Tell him it might be something from the deleted files."

Kate relayed the message and then said to Vail, "He's still not sure, but there is something familiar about it."

"Then tell him I need him back here."

She told him and hung up. "Twenty minutes."

Vail patted the couch next to him, and Kate sat down. He handed her half the Sundra Boston pile. "If it's anywhere, I think it's in here. Somewhere."

Kate started looking through the pages, carefully piling the ones she finished next to her. "Are you sure you saw Longmeadow's name in this case? It just doesn't seem possible that the Russians could be connected to Sundra's disappearance."

"I know, but with that other air force sergeant, Gallagher, also disappearing without a trace, it's something we have to consider."

"But he wasn't the mole. Why would they make him disappear?"

"You weren't a spy, and they tried a different kind of vanishing act on you. Keep looking. If I'm wrong about that name being in here, then there's no connection."

Fifteen minutes later they heard Bursaw come in. He walked into the room and said, "What's going on?"

Vail told him what Kate and Mallon had found at the Pentagon, and that Longmeadow was currently their leading suspect to be Preston. Vail gave him half his remaining stack, and Bursaw started going through it, not even taking the time to pull off his topcoat.

Suddenly Kate said, "Here it is. Toll records for a Chester Longmeadow."

Vail and Bursaw moved closer and read over her shoulder.

Bursaw said, "Then her disappearance has to be connected to the Russians."

"Apparently so. We just have to figure out how." Vail told him about the missing air force sergeant.

"Why are they making these people disappear?"

Vail leaned back and closed his eyes for a few seconds. "There's a hidden level of this that we're not seeing."

"Like what?" Kate asked.

"I don't have the slightest idea, but our neat little explanation for everything so far being caused by old-school Russia versus old-school U.S. isn't going to work anymore. There's a well-camouflaged hand in this."

"Do you mean like an agent provocateur," she asked, "someone trying to use us against our own interests?"

"Something like that. But since we don't know

whether it's a person, a group, or another country, and we don't know what their real purpose is, it's more like an agent X."

"This is getting too big. We're going to need some help," Kate said.

Vail just looked at her in response.

"Shouldn't we at least tell the director?"

"You don't tell *just* the director. There are people he has to inform, and so do they." Vail looked at his watch. "It's too late to get anything done tonight, but first thing in the morning, Luke, we've got to find out if there are more missing people who could be related to this whole thing. You made some contacts when you came up with those missing prostitutes. You're going to have to search Virginia, D.C., and Maryland and look for people with clearances who are missing. If you run into a possible, just check the name in indices, since we should have background-investigation files on them. If they're not in there, move on. Also, it would be nice to know why Sundra was looking at Longmeadow—where that lead came from."

"I'll make some calls."

"Kate and I will get Longmeadow's phone calls broken down and see who he's been calling."

"I assume we're not going to talk to him," Kate said.

"We're not going anywhere near him, his residence, his bank, or his dry cleaner. We need him alive. Luke, let's run this one backward for a while and see what you come up with. In the meantime Kate and I will figure out who's on Longmeadow's speed dial."

Bursaw said, "I should be able to get this done by sometime tomorrow." He got up and left.

Kate was studying Longmeadow's phone records. "We're going to need a subpoena to get information on this many phone numbers. We can sneak one or two by our contact at the phone company, but this is too much."

"Think Tim Mallon can help us out?" Vail asked.

"With the phone company?"

"That guy Hillstrand who took the two kids, didn't I read that he was coming up for trial?"

"Tim did say a hearing had been set for next month and that if Hillstrand didn't plead out, he'd need you and me to testify."

"Then I'm sure the prosecutor is in a frenzy, throwing subpoenas around like confetti. We'll get Tim to piggyback our numbers on one of them. I'm sure there's enough useless information being accumulated right now in the name of justice that you could probably sneak in a request for the invasion plans of North Korea and no one would notice. That's one good thing about a child's kidnapping: People become so emotional that they don't mind bending a few rules. Can you call Tim again?"

"Right now?"

"You said he owed us *two* favors, didn't you?"

"I was thinking more of the misdemeanor variety."

"There is a time for misdemeanors, and there is a time for magnificence."

"You sound like Fagin instructing the Artful Dodger."

"Actually, I think that's from Foghorn Leghorn."

"It doesn't really matter whether it's Dickens or Warner Brothers, the important thing is that it's an irrefutable source."

She found the number on her cell phone and dialed. Vail watched as she walked up and down the length of the room, slightly uncomfortable with what she was about to ask an old friend to do. She had slipped her shoes off and glided as if on skates across the hardwood floors, trying to make the call less rigorous. She laughed at something Mallon said. Her laugh was almost too husky to be feminine, but that's what made it seem genuine to Vail. Finally she made her request of the Reston chief and gave Vail a playful glare as she asked Mallon to falsify the subpoena.

After telling him she'd e-mail the phone numbers they were interested in, she snapped her phone shut at Vail in mild protest. "First thing tomorrow morning, Stan."

"Thank you."

"What else?"

"I think we're both off duty," Vail said.

"I should go get some sleep. There might be other friendships I have to violate, and I don't want to be dozing off during that."

"'Should' makes it sound like you want to be talked out of it."

"Sorry, I'm saving myself."

"For?"

"I think it was Foghorn Leghorn who said it best—'a time for magnificence.'"

He moved close to her and put his arms around

her. With a lopsided grin, he said, "I'll be quick, I promise."

Kate had to be careful not to show how painful it was to maintain her nonchalance. There was nothing she wanted more right now than to accept his offer. "See, there's the problem, bricklayer. Only men equate quickness with magnificence."

THIRTY

WHEN KATE CAME IN THE NEXT MORNING, SHE FOUND VAIL in the kitchen cooking. "Did you eat?" he asked her. He was piling French toast and bacon on a plate.

"It looks like there's only enough for six people, so I won't deprive you. Have you heard from Luke?"

"He's not big on checking in until he's got the answers."

"Too bad you two don't have more in common."

"Did Tim say he'd call?"

"Yes. And he has the fax number here."

Vail sat down and picked up a fork. "You sure?" he asked, pointing at the plate.

"I know that Chicago is 'hog butcher for the world,' but they have heard the rumors about cholesterol there, right?"

"'Stormy, husky, brawling / City of the Big Shoulders.' Does that sound like it was built by men who eat bran muffins?" He stood up and put his arm around her waist. Taking her right hand in his left, he started dancing with her and singing:

I saw a man, he danced with his wife
In Chicago, Chicago, my hometown

After a couple more turns, she stepped back, laughing. "Sit down and eat, you maniac." She watched him for a few seconds. "You're in an awfully good mood."

"Good food, a new mystery, and"—he leaned in close and lowered his voice—"an extremely lusty wench who I suspect I'm about to close the deal with. Life is bountiful."

"Apparently Carl Sandburg forgot to mention dementia in his list of Chicago's attributes." She went over to the counter and poured herself and Vail a cup of coffee. "Anything I can do until we hear from Tim?"

"Maybe you'd better make an appearance at headquarters. We don't need people getting curious."

"I do have a ton of mail that I need to get through, as boring as that suddenly seems."

"Hey, I offered you an alternative. You could be in there right now trying to keep me from falling off one of those army cots, but apparently I'm demented."

"Ah, yes, nothing says romance quite like 'army cot.'"

ABOUT 11:30 A.M. the off-site's phone rang. It was Kate. "Tim just called me. He's faxing the phone information to you."

"I still haven't heard from Luke. Can you get out of there?"

"I'm through about half this mess. If I set fire to the other half, I don't think anything would be lost or I'd be missed."

Vail looked over at the fax machine as it came to life and started printing pages. "We've got incoming facsimiles."

"I'm on my way."

By the time Kate got there, Vail had pinned sheets of paper to a new section of the wall. She went and stood next to him as he studied them. "Anything?"

"Fortunately, Master Sergeant Longmeadow doesn't appear to have many friends. And family, if they do exist, don't appear to be a priority. But he does have a small, inexplicable pattern of calling a car wash."

"A car wash? Who calls a car wash?"

"The phone is listed to the Sunshine Car Wash Company, but according to the utility companies the address comes back to the Lithuanian Chess Society."

"A chess club?"

"They probably figured if the mob could have hunting and fishing clubs, why not chess for them?"

"Do you think they're actually Lithuanian or a front for the Russians?"

"There's only so many things you can find out staring at a wall."

"We're going there, aren't we?" Kate asked.

"I seriously doubt that you dropped everything and ran over here to stay *out* of trouble."

AS KATE NAVIGATED through the crowded traffic of northwest D.C., she said, "This is the Adams Morgan area. Lot of Latinos and West Africans.

And a mix of everything else—and now, I guess, even Lithuanians. Or maybe Russians pretending to be Lithuanians. This is it up on the right."

She parked in front of the address. It was a brick storefront with a long, thin slotted window too high up to see into. There was a small, hand-painted sign affixed to the paneled-steel front door, which read THE LITHUANIAN CHESS SOCIETY. The background was a black-and-white checkerboard pattern. Above it was a peephole and, to the left, a doorbell. "Apparently they're not looking for any walk-in members," Vail said. He rang the bell and held his credentials up to the peephole. Almost immediately he sensed that someone had come to the door and was watching them.

A man in his early fifties opened the door. He was dressed in a suit, and his hair was thick and carefully cut. "FBI?" he said, and stepped back. "Please come in out of the cold." Although his diction was flawless, it didn't take a trained ear to detect he was from somewhere in Eastern Europe. "Are you also with the FBI, miss?"

The question, trying to mitigate its condescension with the courtesy of "miss," was meant to inform this woman, no matter how attractive, of her second-class citizenship inside the walls of the Lithuanian Chess Society. Kate smiled perfectly to relay her understanding of the tactic, and its ineffectiveness. She opened her credentials with an experienced flick of the wrist. Intentionally, she gave no verbal response, enhancing her authority even more.

"I'm Steve Vail, and this is Kate Bannon," Vail

said. "Actually, she's my boss." The man stared at him for a moment and then said, "Alex Zogas." He seemed to be speaking to Vail only, as though still trying not to acknowledge Kate's presence.

Although he knew the answer, Vail asked, "What exactly is this place?"

"This is a social club, but our main interest is chess. Everyone who belongs is a master."

"And Lithuanian?"

"Some of us are, but members come and go. You know how it is."

"And that's all you do here, play chess?"

"We have dinner a few times a week. We come here to get away."

"From?"

"In American homes there are pressures that men from our backgrounds are not accustomed to." Zogas smiled and glanced at Kate. "We come here to commiserate."

"Any chance I can get an application?"

Zogas laughed. "I don't know. If you are Lithuanian, it would help."

"Unfortunately, I have no idea what my heritage is. My father was always wanted by the law, so we were continuously changing names. The only thing I know for sure is that I'm a citizen of the United States."

"As are all of us, if that's what you are trying to find out with your little 'antibiography,' shall we say."

Vail grinned. "That was one of my curiosities."

"And the others are . . . ?" Zogas asked.

"I was wondering if there was any business purpose to your group."

"Other than members networking, no, none. This is strictly social."

"Are you the only one here now?"

"No, there are others in the back if you'd like to talk to them," Zogas offered. "Mind if I ask why you're here?"

Vail held out a photo of Sundra Boston. "She's why. Ever seen her?"

Zogas looked at it and said, "Around here? We discourage having members bring women in. Who is she?"

"Her name is Sundra Boston, and she works for the FBI. She's missing."

"Why would you look for her here?"

"Apparently she was looking into your club's activities."

"Chess?"

"She's a financial analyst," Vail lied.

"We collect dues from which our monthly expenses are paid. That's the only thing financial about our club. You're welcome to look at our accounts. It's all on the computer in the office, if it'll help clear this up."

"It would be nice if things were that simple. But we'll have a look."

Zogas gave Vail an inadvertent smirk. "Back this way." He led them through a large room that had a half-dozen tables with chessboards embedded in their tops, two of which were being used. None of the four men looked up at the agents as they walked through.

In the very back of the club were two smaller rooms, one a bathroom, the other an office, which

Zogas led them into. Then he turned on the computer. Vail noticed a chessboard on a small table next to the desk. A game appeared to be in progress, but there was no room for a chair on the opposite side. "A game by mail?" Vail asked.

"Yes. Do you play?"

"I played for a couple of months in college. Very intently, but I just didn't have the patience for it."

"That's too bad. For someone in your line of work, it could be an asset." After opening up a file marked "Club Expenses," Zogas got up and offered Vail the chair. Kate moved behind him.

He scrolled through the last two years' entries, which showed a balance that was usually in the black, occasionally crossing into the red at the end of the month. He looked up at Zogas. "Pretty boring stuff."

"We are men who find chess fascinating. Did you expect our lives to be secretly interesting?"

"I must have missed something when I tried it. What is it about chess that you find so intriguing?"

"Are you familiar with the term 'zero sum'? It is from game theory. It means that someone has to win and someone has to lose. We find it a welcome relief from the constant compromising of present-day America and its obsession with equality."

"That has been this country's downfall," Vail said. "As far as you know, none of your members have had any contact with the FBI, for any reason?"

"Not that I'm aware of," Zogas said. "How would our name come up in one of your investigations?"

"I guess that's the real question, isn't it?" Vail wasn't going to tell Zogas that it was Longmeadow's phone records, in case someone knew him and might warn him. It was a long shot, but he didn't like the Lithuanian's calculated responses to his questions, so he decided that a couple of lies would give Zogas something to think about. "The woman I showed you a picture of did all kinds of investigations. Sometimes institutional irregularities came to her attention, sometimes people called in tips, and sometimes something was a spin-off of another investigation. The notes she left behind indicated that she was just getting started on the LCS—sorry, that was her shorthand for your club, or society if you prefer—so there wasn't much detailed information. Do you have any enemies who might have called the FBI about your club?"

"No."

"How about any bad business deals away from the club? What kind of businesses are your members involved in?"

"Nothing very exotic. We are all successful, with varying interests. It's kind of an unwritten requirement for membership here, to be financially established. I, for example, own eight coin-operated car washes in the D.C. area. They're all self-serve, so my time to run them is minimal. Others have dry-cleaning stores, car rentals, and hair-cutting shops. One of our members even does some translating for the government in immigration cases. Certainly nothing that would be cause for retribution against a group of men whose passion is chess."

"Well, this just may be one of those times that a mystery has to remain a mystery. Do you mind if I show the others the woman's photo?"

"Please do."

They walked back into the game room. Zogas spoke with the vague authority of a leader. "These people are from the FBI. They have a photograph of a missing woman who also worked for the FBI and was apparently looking into our club's activities." There was no reaction from any of the four men, none of them even looking up. Vail glanced at Kate to confirm the oddity of their lack of response.

Vail went over to the first table and showed the photograph. "Her name is Sundra Boston. Have you ever seen or heard of her?" Both men shook their heads in silence.

At the second table, Vail showed the photograph again, and after the two men glanced at it, he continued to study their faces. They both appeared to have dark circles around their eyes and mouths. "I'm sorry, you seem familiar," Vail said to the one who hardly looked at the photo. "Have we met before?"

Slowly the man raised his eyes to Vail. In a controlled tone, he answered, "No." Even though a single syllable, Vail could hear its heavy accent.

"I'm sorry, what is your name?"

The man glanced at Zogas, who gave an almost undetectable nod. "Algis Barkus."

Vail smiled. "No, I guess not. I would have remembered that name. Everyone, thank you for your time."

Zogas walked them to the front door. "If there is anything else we can do for you, please do not hesitate to ask."

"There is one thing that would help put this to

rest. Do you think we could get a list of your membership?"

For the first time since their entering the club, Zogas appeared to be caught flat-footed. "That might be a problem."

"Why?" Vail asked, almost before Zogas finished.

"We have worked extremely hard since coming to this country and taking citizenship. We enjoy having this sanctuary and, in relative anonymity, being allowed to socialize with men of similar interests. This is a small but, we feel, elite group. I doubt that the membership would approve of the U.S. government knowing exactly who we are. We fear that it wouldn't be long before someone from some governmental agency would be demanding we admit two Hispanics, four females, and someone in a wheelchair."

"We're only looking for a quick way to cross you off our list of people who might know something about one of our employees disappearing. We're not going to turn your membership roster over to Health and Human Services."

"I'll tell you what, Agent Vail. I will present your argument to the members, and they'll put it to a vote."

"How long will that take?"

"A day, two at the most."

"I'll call you. Is there a number here?"

Zogas took out a business card and wrote it on the back. "Give me two days. By then I should have a definitive answer."

For the first time since entering the club, Vail heard the men in the back speak. He listened for a moment and then asked, "Is that Lithuanian?"

"Yes, it is."

"Interesting. People, probably myself included, have a tendency to lump all the Eastern European languages together. But it is definitely different from, say, Russian." Vail watched him closely to see if "Russian" hit any nerves.

"You have a good ear. They are definitely different languages."

Once they were outside, Kate said, "I guess we've solved one mystery today. Now we know the where-abouts of Himmler's, Goebbels's and Göring's sons." When Vail didn't laugh, she thought that his mind had once again raced ahead, trying to find the next turn. She glanced at him and saw something in his face she'd never seen before. He actually looked shaken. "Steve, what is it?"

He turned and searched her face as if he didn't know who she was. Then he said, "I know who framed you."

THIRTY-ONE

WHAT!"

When Vail didn't answer, Kate asked again. "What did you say?"

"Not here." He grabbed her by the arm and glanced back at the club, pushing her toward their car.

He started the engine, and she asked again, "What is it?"

Still he wouldn't answer but pulled away from the curb and drove off, once more checking to see if anyone from the club was watching. When he got a block away and was certain that none of the Lithuanians could see them, he pulled over. "That night you and I broke into the Russian safe house in Denton, remember?"

"Guys in ski masks, large handguns, you setting off explosives, fire—something about it rings a bell."

"Did you notice anything funny about that guy Barkus or the other one playing chess with him?"

"Other than their warmth toward FBI agents, especially the female subspecies, not really," she said. "Oh, Barkus had dark circles under his eyes.

Probably something to do with his not getting back to the coffin until after sunrise."

"You weren't as close to him as I was. Or the other one. They both had them, dark circles all the way around their eyes—and around their mouths, too."

"What were they?"

"Dozens of tiny cuts scabbed over."

"The areas left exposed by ski masks. From the shattered lightbulbs," Kate said.

"And that night they were speaking in some foreign language that wasn't Russian. It sounded Eastern European. It could have been Lithuanian. It all makes sense now. That guy in the tunnel in Chicago, Jonas Sakis, he made a reference to game theory and zero-sum games. And when I said something about him being Russian, he gave me this strange smirk. It was because he was Lithuanian."

"That means—oh, my God!" Kate said. "That means these guys are tied directly to the Russians. They're working with them, and they have ears and eyes in the NSA, the CIA, the Pentagon, the State Department, and who knows where else."

"That's why we've got to be very careful. You, me, and Luke, no one else."

"*No one else?* The three of us against all of them?"

Vail ignored Kate's plea. "The real question is, what's the connection between the Lithuanians and Sundra—and you?"

She shook her head in disbelief at his self-control, gaining her own calm from it. "Connected how?" she asked.

"I don't know, but I got the feeling that the

Lithuanian Chess Society is going to vote nay to our getting a membership list. So let's drive around here while you write down as many tags as possible. Maybe we can identify some of them." Vail put the car in gear, and said, "There was also something Zogas said that bothers me."

"What?"

"You're familiar with statement analysis?"

"A little bit. It's been years since I used it at OPR."

"Do you remember what he said in his announcement to the others about Sundra?"

"No."

"I told him that she *works* for the FBI. He told them that we had a photograph of a missing woman who had *worked* for the FBI. Past tense."

"Couldn't that just be a translation problem for him?"

"It could be. He had an accent, but his grammar was almost flawless. Anyone who uses words like 'commiserate' or can explain game theory in a few words or think of something like 'antibiography' has a better command of English than I do."

"Then that's not a good omen for Sundra, is it?" Kate asked rhetorically.

WHEN THEY PULLED up at the off-site, they saw Bursaw's car parked in front. "Good, Luke's here. Maybe he can help figure this out."

In the workroom they filled Bursaw in on everything that had happened and their conclusion that the LCS was somehow connected to both Sundra

Boston's disappearance and Kate's being framed. Vail explained about Zogas's possible slip in verb tense concerning the well-being of the missing analyst.

Bursaw considered it for a moment. "More often than not, that stuff is accurate. I hope it *was* just a translation problem. I'd like to think we haven't been looking for a dead body."

Vail handed him the list of license plates Kate had taken down at the chess club. "Can you get these run, but not through WFO? Have the locals run them and keep it quiet."

"That detective from Metro Homicide we turned Jonathan Wilkins over to said if I ever needed anything. I've known him for a while, so it won't be a problem to keep it quiet."

"Until we figure it out, we don't need to be distracted by who might know what. You, Kate, and me—that's it. If something leaks out, we won't have to waste time wondering if someone from the Bureau innocently mentioned it to someone that they shouldn't have. We'll know it's something the opposition somehow came up with on their own and we can trace it back that way," Vail said. "How'd you do with the missing persons?"

"I found only one. Maurice Lyle Gaston, late of Matrix-Linx International, Springfield, Virginia. We did a security clearance on him. Matrix-Linx has a defense contract. The only fly in the ointment was that he disappeared in Las Vegas. A sister who lives here reported him missing to Fairfax County when he failed to come back from a weekend getaway there."

"Las Vegas. Interesting." Vail wrote down the information in a small notebook. "Good. Kate and I will look into it."

"On a more definitive note, I did find out how Longmeadow came up in her files."

"How?"

Bursaw smiled as if he were about to unveil an important piece of the puzzle. "In a counterintelligence case. Surveillance was following a Russian by the name of Dimitri Polakov. He was later expelled from the U.S. for suspected spying activities. It was Labor Day, last year, and a surveillance team was looking for a target to follow around. They had no reason to believe he was doing anything—they just wanted to log enough hours to qualify for holiday pay. You know, before they *lost* him and had no choice but to break off the surveillance and go home. All of a sudden, this guy coasts up to a mailbox and then takes off. The team leader sees there's a signal chalked on the box, so now they realize that they've stumbled onto something. There was going to be a drop. Polakov drives all over for the next two hours and lands at an apple orchard that's open to the public—you know, to pick your own apples. The target gets out of his car and wanders off down one of the paths. The crew goes into the parking lot, and they start copping tags, hoping that whoever he's meeting has a car there. They write down fourteen of them. Meanwhile two agents follow Polakov on foot, but he never makes a drop or picks any apples, so the team thinks that they may have gotten burned. But still they had the plates. Maybe one of the tags belongs to whomever Polakov was supposed to meet. They give all of them to Sundra to look into. Subsequently she was just running out the leads by the numbers when she requested tolls on the owners of the cars in the lot. One of them was Chester Alvin Longmeadow."

"So he was there for a drop but probably made the surveillance, and the exchange never took place. That's nice work, Luke," Vail said. "It ties Sundra to Longmeadow, who we now know is connected to the LCS through the sergeant's phone records. And we know that the Lithuanians are connected to the Russians because of their coming to the safe house in Denton."

Bursaw held up the list of license plates collected at the chess club. "I'll head over to Metro and get these run."

After he left, Kate said, "Well, it looks like we've got all the players. Now we just have to figure out how they fit together."

"That's why I thought the three of us should sit down and brainstorm this."

"You're going to wait until Luke comes back?"

"Actually, I thought we'd enlist the help of Sakichi Toyoda."

"Who's that?"

"He was considered the king of Japanese inventors, at least in the early twentieth century. He started a little company called Toyota," Vail said. "But more important, at least for us, he developed the concept of the Five Whys. Ever heard of it?"

"I don't think so."

"Toyoda figured out that when a problem occurs, if you ask why five times, give or take, you'll trace any problem back to its root cause and then can prevent it from recurring."

"I'm not sure I understand."

"Let me give you an example. You have a business manufacturing and selling porcelain dog figurines. One day your customers start calling to complain that the items they received all have the same damage. Let's say the left ear has a crack in it. So you ask *why* are they arriving in that condition? That's one. You find that every one was shipped that way. So, through a series of whys, you discover—number two—that they're coming out of the mold like that because the mold tears during the injection process. And—number three—that's happening because the person who's operating the machine isn't calibrating it properly. Why hasn't he been calibrating it? Number four—because he's new and he didn't know he was supposed to. And—number five—why didn't he know? Because it wasn't part of his training. So you make it a requirement that anyone performing that task has to receive x number of hours of training. Problem solved and, in all likelihood, permanently."

"So if we can answer enough whys, we can figure all this out?"

"I suppose if a person can answer enough questions, he can figure out anything. This is not easy to do. It takes a lot of discipline, a lot of looking at the big picture and the small picture at the same time. However, it does have a way of cutting through the layers of distraction, which in this case are everywhere. If we can do it, we might find a starting point."

"Okay, what's the first why?"

Vail moved to a wall adjoining the one with the documents pinned to it. "I think you've already asked that." With a black marker, he wrote:

1. Why would the LCS be connected to Sundra,
the safe house, & the Calculus list?

Kate said, "Shouldn't that be 'How'?"

"The important thing is to pursue answers to the questions. Toyoda probably wasn't an English major, but he was a genius. Out of respect, let's just use his whys."

"Sorry." Kate thought for a second. "The LCS has to be working with the Russians."

"That's the only possible explanation, with them coming after us in that safe house. And now we can trace Sundra back to Longmeadow, who we know is spying for the Russians. But Lithuanians, historically, have never been fond of the Russians. In fact, Lithuania was the first of the Soviet states to declare its independence after the fall of the Berlin Wall. So . . ." Vail wrote:

2. Why would the LCS and the Russians be working
together?

"I don't know, why?"

"What's always the best guess for motive? Someone wrote a song about it making the world go round?"

"I'm guessing it's not love, so you think this is about money?"

"Very few things aren't. Zogas described himself as a businessman. He said they all own small businesses. They're entrepreneurs. When the Russians need somebody taken out, they call the LCS and are able to keep their own hands clean. If that is true, it brings us to 'why' number three. If the Russians are paying the LCS . . ." He wrote:

3. Why do the Russians want their moles dead?

Kate thought about it for a second. "Like we've been saying all along, it doesn't make any sense, because historically the Russians have always done everything to help their double agents escape to Russia or some other communist country."

"That's a good point. And it brings us to the next why." Turning to the wall, he wrote:

4. Why didn't they kill Rellick immediately?

Studying the wall, Kate said, "We haven't really answered number three yet, have we?"

"No, we haven't. I think we need to consider both questions together. That Rellick was the exception might answer why the others weren't given the option to escape."

Kate said, "The whole point of framing me was to protect Rellick. Maybe he was that valuable to them. Maybe they thought that once he was safely in Russia, he would have been some sort of monument to Russian ingenuity and American decadence."

"Let's assume you're right, or at least partially

right. That leaves one last unanswered question."
He wrote:

5. *Why are other people with security clearances,*
   who are not spies, disappearing?

"First the air force sergeant and now—for the
sake of argument—let's assume that Maurice
Gaston with Matrix-Linx International is also part
of this," Vail said.

"At this point that doesn't seem like much of a
stretch."

"No, it doesn't," he said mechanically, his voice
already slipping away. Vail took a chair from the
desk and rolled it over in front of the wall. He sat
down, and his face dissolved into a reflective blank.
Kate lowered herself onto the couch to wait, occasionally glancing at the questions and trying to
guess where Vail's mind was at the moment.

Almost fifteen minutes later, Vail stood up out
of his chair. "There's only one possibility—at least
that I can think of. The LCS isn't killing these
people for the Russians, they're doing it to protect
themselves."

"From what?"

"This is the age of outsourcing. They saw the
need for a new service industry and offered it to
the Russians. This is also the age of incompetence
in government. Maybe the SVR wasn't recruiting
sources like the old KGB had, and Moscow was
pressuring them to find a solution. The LCS is a
full-service intelligence enterprise. Not only will

they kill someone for you, but they also recruit informants for the Russians."

"What makes you think that?"

"Two things. First, that's why they've been killing their own moles when we get close. They're afraid they may talk if we get them in custody, and once it's exposed, that would be the end of what I'm guessing is a very lucrative business venture for the Lithuanians. It's the only way to explain the two missing people. If you're going to go out and recruit people to betray their country, chances are you're not going to be one hundred percent successful. So if the LCS approaches someone and they're turned down, what would they be most afraid of?"

"Their recruit going to the FBI."

"And the LCS can't have that. So if you refuse, you lose—your life."

"They can't be approaching these people cold and expecting them to turn," Kate said.

"You're right, they're probably not. The key is Gaston disappearing in Las Vegas. Where better to compromise someone than a place with unlimited liquor, gambling, women, and desperation?"

"So they're blackmailing them into giving up classified secrets."

"That's the only way everything makes sense. I suppose they may occasionally get a lead on someone who's heavily in debt or overleveraged with the bookies, but I think their tool of choice is most likely extortion. It's as old as spying itself. Another advantage to it is that if you're just an everyday double agent for the Russians, you can quit anytime you want to, but if our Lithuanian chess players have got something on you, you're in forever."

"So these people they recruit aren't being paid?"

"Once they're compromised, and probably re-corded, the LCS owns them. I'd guess they're given a small percentage of what the Russians pay. At this point I think we can safely assume that Long-meadow is Preston. Remember what he said on the tape: 'This time I want a hundred thousand dollars in cash, just for me.' In other words, he's tired of sharing. He wasn't talking to his Russian handler, he was negotiating with an LCS extortionist."

Now it was Kate who stared at the five questions on the wall. She filtered them all through Vail's conclusions. Finally she said, "You're making some leaps, but I can't think of anything to disprove it. It does all fit."

"For the moment."

"Meaning?"

"This *is* all supposition. They know that the only way we can prove any of this is by turning the people they've recruited. That's why they've been killing them as soon as we get close."

"So they've destroyed all the potential witnesses against them."

"Not all of them. We have Longmeadow, who evidently they think we've missed so they're leaving him be."

"Then why don't we go get him and see if he'll come clean? If he is being blackmailed, he'd prob-ably be glad to get them off his back."

"Two things. First, we have no evidence other than that brief recorded conversation, and I'm not sure we could prove it's his voice or that there's any real spying involved. Second, every time we've gone anywhere near one of these people, they wound up dead. The LCS has some early-warning system in place. Until we can figure out what it is and how to get around it, I think we should let him be. With Rellick dead, they probably think we're satisfied that everything has been put to rest. A couple of days isn't going to make any difference. This is another advantage to our not telling anyone else; we don't have to worry about it leaking out while we wait."

"And in the meantime . . . ?"

"The routine stuff. We'll try to find out if they recruited someone else from Matrix-Linx after Gaston disappeared, like they did with the air force. We've got the advantage now. They don't know we're coming."

"You don't think our little trip to their clubhouse will force them to tie up loose ends like Long-meadow?"

"With Rellick dead, I'm hoping not. They've killed all the evidence, remember? But if they do get nervous, they'll have no option but to play defense, and that might mean eliminating all loose ends."

Kate asked, "Aren't we loose ends?"

"These people aren't fools. The easiest way to prevent Rellick from being exposed would have been to kill you. . . ."

Again Vail's thoughts were drifting in another direction. This time she couldn't wait. "What?"

"Your suicide attempt."

"My what? You knew about that?"

Absentmindedly, Vail said, "The director told

me about it. That's how he got me to change my mind downstairs that day."

"You believed I would try to commit suicide?"

"Over you dumping me, yeah, that makes sense. He told me that your reputation was being questioned. I know how small-minded these people can be. He thought that if you and I could resolve the Calculus list, the rumors would be put to rest."

"And you never told me? Why? And why would you go through all this if you didn't believe it? You were almost killed—more than once."

He grabbed her roughly by her arm and pulled her against him. His lips were almost touching hers. His breathing quickened. "Aren't you ever going to get this?"

THIRTY-TWO

UNSURE WHERE IT WOULD TAKE THEM—AND NOT SURE SHE cared—Kate touched her lips lightly to Vail's.

Suddenly the door downstairs opened. She drew her head back and, with her voice unintentionally throaty, said, "That's Luke."

"Luke who?"

She put her head on his chest. "I wish I could remember."

She started to move away, and Vail pulled her hand to his mouth, nipping the skin at the back of it. "What idiot gave him a key?"

As soon as Bursaw walked in, he sensed he'd interrupted something. "I . . . uh, forgot something in the car," he offered diplomatically. "I'll be right back."

"That's all right, Luke. We were just finishing an argument," Kate said playfully.

Bursaw noticed the new handwriting on the wall and went over to it. "Is there one answer to all five questions?"

"We think the LCS is doing contract recruitment of sources for the Russians. Using blackmail when they can."

Bursaw reread the questions and Vail's terse,

cryptic answers. After a minute he said, "Impressive. Logically, it does answer all the questions."

Vail turned to Kate. "We must be right. Philosophers take a death oath to never agree with any definitive conclusion."

Bursaw said, "I guess the challenge is proving it?"

"That's what we were trying to figure out."

"Do you think Sundra was approached?" Bursaw asked.

"Hard to say, but my guess would be that they found out she was making inquiries about Longmeadow. Somewhere it leaked out. Maybe, like us, she picked up on all the calls to car washes and started making inquiries into Zogas's businesses and he got wind of it. We may never know now. If they approached her, maybe she was offered money to shut her up. It wouldn't have been hard for them to find out how much debt she was in. If they offered her something and she refused, their only option left would be to make her disappear, along with her computer files."

Bursaw turned around, and the anger he was trying to suppress was obvious. "So she *was* just doing her job."

"Her problem was that she was doing more than her job. Don't worry, Luke, we're going to settle this, I promise. But right now we all need to be cool."

Bursaw took a few seconds and then nodded. "I'm okay." He opened his briefcase and removed a stack of papers. "I had those plates run and got only a couple of hits." He smiled more calmly now. "But I had an idea. The few plates that came back to them all listed the club's address, so I had this gal I know at DMV security run an offline search for all vehicles registered at that address for the last three years." He handed Vail a sheet of paper. "Everyone from Alex Zogas on down. Eight altogether."

Vail scanned the list. There was Algis Barkus, who'd had the cuts around his eyes at the club, and one other that Vail found very interesting. "Jonas Sakis." Vail turned the list so Kate could see it. "The guy who tried to kill me in Chicago."

She said, "Then two of them are probably the guys you and John shot in Annandale."

"Which would mean we're down to five."

"So what do we do now? Sit on the club?" Bursaw asked. "We don't have a home address for any of them."

"They'll be looking for us there. No, I was thinking that my car needed washing." Bursaw looked at him questioningly. "Zogas owns car washes. His machines have money in them. You don't think a good businessman would leave them full overnight, do you?"

"I'll go with you."

"Let me change into some surveillance clothes," Vail said. "Kate, you want to come along?"

"Surveillance? You mean me watching you sleep? As enjoyable as that would be, it'll be slightly less boring if I get back to the office and put another dent in that paperwork. You'll call me if you get anything?"

"Only if there's going to be shooting involved."

• • •

ALEX ZOGAS HAD been brooding since the FBI left, and he hadn't said a dozen words. The other four men knew not to say anything when he was like that. At the moment he was playing chess against Algis Barkus, and Barkus could tell by his distracted play that Zogas was planning something. Although he'd told the agents that all the men of the Lithuanian Chess Society were chess masters, only Zogas was, and right now Barkus was playing him even. It was part of Zogas's planning process. There was something about the discipline of the game that he used to unravel and reassemble the most complicated problems. Finally he shifted in his seat, redirecting his concentration to the board, and almost immediately made a brazen move, straightening up and smiling confidently. Whatever the problem was, it had been solved, and Zogas was now less than a handful of moves from checkmate.

It was Zogas's fourth move that caused Barkus to tip his king over in surrender. Zogas got up and went to the office. The men could hear him typing on the computer. A couple minutes later, he came back and gave Barkus a slip of paper with an address on it. "Nine o'clock. Meet me there." Zogas nodded at a second man playing chess, Bernard Mindera, to go with him. Short and powerfully built, Mindera seemed pleased to be chosen and started picking up his chess pieces from the board.

IT WAS AFTER 8 P.M., and the temperature had fallen well below freezing. Vail and Bursaw sat parked at a discreet distance from one of Alex Zogas's Sunshine car washes. "Man, I can't believe that in the dead of winter so many people stand out in the cold to wash their cars," Bursaw said.

"It does seem like a license to steal."

A silver Lincoln pulled in and parked in an out-of-the-way spot that precluded the possibility of its being there for a wash. The two agents watched the well-dressed man get out and tug up the collar on his topcoat. "That's Zogas," Vail said.

There were three washing bays, and they watched as Zogas emptied each of the machines of the day's receipts and put them into a canvas bag. "I had my doubts," Bursaw said, "but you were right about him not wanting to leave the money overnight."

Zogas got back into his car and waited for a break in the traffic. Vail said, "I assume you can follow him without getting made."

"Although I should never bet against you when food is at stake, dinner says I can."

"Why do I get the feeling that my supper to-night is going to be at some drive-through?"

The Lincoln pulled into traffic heading north.

"Any idea where he might be going, Steve?"

"I'm just hoping he leads us to where he lives. We have no background on this guy at all. With a residence we can get a phone number and all kinds of other information."

They followed him to a second Sunshine Car Wash, and Bursaw, once again, set up down the street.

After a third car wash, Zogas drove to a bank and

parked in the lot. He sat in the car for a while before Bursaw said, "Looks like he's counting money and filling out a deposit slip."

"I do believe we have found where he does his banking. Those records should be interesting."

Finally Zogas got out of his car and walked over to the night depository, using a key to open it. On the way back, he checked his wristwatch. "Looks like he's got something scheduled. It's after eight thirty, kind of late. Maybe it's spy stuff," Bursaw said.

"Wouldn't that be nice?"

The Lincoln pulled back into traffic, and Bursaw waited for a couple of cars to get between them before easing into the same lane. "He's driving too slow. Think he's early for an appointment?"

They had been traveling southeast for almost twenty minutes when they reached Temple Hills. Zogas parked outside a large apartment complex. The two agents watched as he turned off the ignition and dialed his cell phone. "What do you think, Steve?"

"I have no idea. We've just got to stay with him." They could see him dialing a second number now. After a minute he hung up, started his car, and made a U-turn. Vail and Bursaw looked at each other questioningly. Bursaw turned the Bureau car around and maintained his distance behind the Lincoln again. They followed him for almost a half hour to an upscale neighborhood in Capitol Heights, where he pulled into a three-car garage and then closed the door. Vail made a note of the address.

"So now we know his bank and home address. Not a bad night's work," Bursaw said.

But Vail didn't answer. Bursaw glanced at him. He was sitting with his head back and his eyes closed. Finally Vail said, "Why did he go to Temple Hills to make a couple of phone calls?"

"Maybe he didn't want to call from his home because he's worried about us getting a fix on what cell tower he was running off of. You know these people always think we have more capabilities than we do."

"Maybe," Vail said. He took out a map book of the greater D.C. area. After studying it for a few seconds, he said, "Do you know what's less than two miles from where he stopped in Temple Hills? Andrews Air Force Base. Where does Longmeadow live?"

Bursaw reached into the backseat and retrieved his briefcase. He shuffled through the papers and pulled out Longmeadow's information. "His current address is in Camp Springs, Virginia."

Vail looked back at the map. "It's adjacent to the base, less than two miles from where Zogas made the calls. They're going to kill Longmeadow."

THIRTY-THREE

As THEY NEARED THE ADDRESS FOR MASTER SERGEANT Longmeadow's apartment, Vail spotted one of the cars he'd seen at the chess club. There were two men in the front seat. "Luke, there! The guy driving is the one who calls himself Barkus."

Bursaw waited until there was a little more distance between them before making a U-turn. "Think they saw us?"

"A black guy with a white guy, in this car? I wouldn't be optimistic."

"Do you want to try to stop them?"

"Not yet. If they did kill Longmeadow, he's either in his apartment or in that car. If it's the car, then we want to see where they're going with the body."

Bursaw knew what Vail wasn't saying. Wherever they were heading, if Longmeadow's body was in the car, they were taking it to someplace they considered safe to dump bodies. Maybe that was where Sundra was.

Vail picked up the mike and radioed the Washington Field Office. "We are following a car with two men who may have just committed a homicide. We need you to call the Camp Springs PD and have them immediately check the following location for a victim." Vail gave them Longmeadow's address and apartment number.

Bursaw continued to follow the car at a discreet distance, keeping at least two other vehicles between them. "Looks like they're heading for 495."

Vail didn't say anything but continued to watch the car closely. It exited onto 495 and then 95 South. "Notice anything funny about the way they're driving?"

"It's by the book. Signaling lane changes, right at the speed limit."

"Who drives like that?" Vail said.

"Someone who doesn't want to get stopped. I'm guessing the late Chester Longmeadow is aboard."

For the next fifteen minutes, they followed the car driven by Algis Barkus. As the traffic thinned out, Bursaw was able to lengthen the distance between it and his Bureau vehicle. Suddenly the WFO radio operator's voice cut through the air. *The Camp Springs PD just called back. They had the manager let them into the apartment, and it was empty. There were no signs of a struggle or that anything unusual had taken place.*

"Copy, Central," Vail said, and leaned back. "I guess we're on the way to a burial."

The area was more rural now and the road darker. Bursaw was able to drop back even farther. "Think we should call for some help? We're getting close to the Richmond office's turf."

"The whole point is to follow these two until we find where they're going to dump the body. The chances of someone jumping into the middle of a surveillance in progress and not getting burned are about zero."

Barkus signaled that he was exiting off the highway and onto Route 30. "Too late now," Bursaw said. He turned onto the ramp for 30 East. "Here we go."

Once they were on Route 30, Bursaw closed the gap between them. They had gone less than ten miles when Barkus turned right onto a dirt road. Bursaw slowed to let the distance increase, since it would be harder to go unnoticed in such an isolated spot. The road was little more than a trail, narrow and barely passable. Bursaw slowed the Bureau car to a crawl and switched his headlights to parking lights.

There was no illumination from the main road, but the moon had risen and was providing some light through the partially cloudy sky. The road wound around, and with their headlights off, the two agents didn't notice an overgrown path off to the right, which Barkus had turned his vehicle into. The Lithuanian had then made a left-hand turn and switched off his lights and engine, leaving him invisible as Bursaw went by with his parking lights now off. Barkus rolled down his window and listened. Once he heard the FBI car go by, he started the engine, backed up onto the dirt road, then shut the car off again, blocking the road so the agents couldn't drive out of the woods.

Without a word both men got out and went to the trunk. They shoved the heavy canvas bag containing Longmeadow's body to the side and took out night goggles, putting them on quickly. Ironically, Longmeadow had given Zogas the thermal-imaging devices when trying to demonstrate to him the utility of the larger system he was about to sell him the secrets to. Then they took out Russian-made Bison submachine guns, chambering the first round. Positioning themselves behind the car, they waited for Vail and Bursaw to drive back.

A hundred yards farther down the curving road, Bursaw hit the brakes. They were at the beach of a small lake. At one end of the sand was a dock with a ladder leading down into the water, presumably for getting on and off small boats. "Where did they go?" Bursaw asked.

"We must have missed some turnoff, but I didn't see anything other than an overgrown path."

"Think this is where the bodies wound up?"

"If it is, then why aren't they down here?" Vail said. "You'd better go back."

It took Bursaw a couple of passes before he could completely turn the car around. He still hadn't switched his headlights back on, but he drove a little faster in case the two men from the LCS had used the maneuver to lose them. He came around the curve and almost hit Barkus's car before slamming to a stop. "What the—"

Bursaw's unfinished question was answered by automatic fire that ricocheted off the front of the Bureau car. In the muzzle flashes, Vail could see that the men were wearing night-vision goggles. After the first burst, the two gunmen ran from behind the car and into the woods to get some flanking fire into the vehicle from a vantage point where they wouldn't have to fire through the engine block. Both agents saw where they were going and scrambled out of the passenger-side door. "Do you think they made the surveillance?" Vail asked.

"I'd go ask them if I spoke Lithuanian." Another burst of fire raked the car, taking out the driver's-side windows.

"I don't suppose you have anything useful in the trunk, like a SWAT team."

"Just a shotgun."

"Did you see the goggles? They're thermal-imaging."

Bursaw waited a moment for some explanation as to how that was going to help them and then said, "What a fun fact, Mr. Science."

"As soon as they figure out that we only have handguns, they're going to fire and maneuver until they can get around our car, and we'll be sharing a three-body condo with Longmeadow. Go back by the trunk. As soon as you hear them firing at me, look and see where it's coming from. Then start firing in that direction. Take your time, empty a clip—but slowly. As soon as you finish, I'll take off. Those goggles have a very narrow field of vision. I'll fire at them, and they'll see only me, but they'll think we're still together. Then get under the car toward the front. With the engine still running, there'll be a billowing heat signature down there, and they won't be able to distinguish you from the car. They'll chase after me, thinking we're together. Once they do, take the shotgun out and get down to the water as fast as possible."

Vail took off his jacket and pulled off his black sweatshirt, putting the coat back on against the freezing cold. He took out his pocketknife and cut two slits into the shirt.

"You're going down to the water?"

"Something like that. Once you hear gunfire down there, or me yelling . . . well, you can figure it out from there. Just remember, I'll be the guy *without* the goggles."

"There's no place to hide down there."

"Sure there is," Vail said. "You ready?"

Bursaw moved to the back of the car. "Ready."

Vail stood up, and almost immediately automatic-weapons fire raked the opposite side of the car as he ducked down again. Bursaw leaned across the trunk and fired in a slow rhythm.

As soon as he finished, Vail took off, firing a couple of shots to attract the two gunmen's attention. Bursaw scrambled under the car and waited, his handgun reloaded and ready.

When Vail reached the beach, he ran out onto the pier. At the end, by the ladder, he carefully placed his Glock at the edge. Then, without hesitation, he jumped down, breaking through the thin layer of ice covering the lake. Using the ladder to keep himself under, he held his breath in the freezing water that bit into his skin like hot needles. He held a finger to his carotid artery and timed his heart rate. If he and Bursaw were going to get out of there alive, he was going to have to induce the initial stages of hypothermia to lower his body's heat signature. After the run, his heart rate was at fifty-two. After a minute and a half, it had dropped to forty.

He raised his head out of the water and listened. He could hear the two men yelling to each other, working their way through the woods toward the beach. He lowered his head back into the water and waited.

When his heart rate hit thirty-six, he began to shiver uncontrollably, another sure sign of hypothermia. He started feeling light-headed and knew he was on his way to losing consciousness.

Slowly, so the dripping water couldn't be heard, he climbed the ladder, picked up his automatic, and shoved it in the back of his waistband. Then he crawled onto the dock, placing the black shirt over his head and positioning it so he could see through the slits he had cut. He lay still with his hands underneath him and waited for his clothing to freeze. He was shivering violently.

Less than a minute later, Barkus and Mindera stepped onto the beach searching for the agents, looking as much at the woods behind them as in the direction of the water.

The two men were speaking Lithuanian and sounded as though they were both now on the sand. Vail closed his eyes and put his head down so they wouldn't be able to detect the heat coming through the eye slits in his shirt.

Hopefully Bursaw had survived, but Vail couldn't depend on that. Then he heard one of their voices coming closer, almost as if it were aimed at him. Vail knew that besides the narrow field of vision of the thermal goggles, they had one other disadvantage: everything that didn't give off heat appeared green and lumped together, almost completely indistinguishable. Vail was depending on that one shortcoming, but he quickly became less confident when he felt one of his pursuer's step onto the rickety pier and heard him yell something to the other man in Lithuanian that had the unmistakable tone of discovery in it.

Suddenly there was an explosion from the edge of the woods. A single booming shotgun blast was fired in the direction of the voices. And another. Both the Lithuanians wheeled and fired at the large tree where Bursaw was taking cover. Vail got to his feet and, still almost paralyzed with the cold, squeezed his handgun tighter than he ever had before. He fired three rounds at the man closest to him, some fifteen feet away. The body thudded lifelessly onto the pier.

Vail hurried to him, ripped off the goggles, and put them on. He could see that the second man, thinking Vail's shots were his partner's, was moving quickly toward the tree that protected Bursaw. As he moved to within a few feet of the tree, Vail dropped to one knee, held his breath, and emptied his magazine, aiming as best he could with his hands and body shaking furiously. The Lithuanian went down, and Vail stood up, ramming another magazine from his belt into the pistol, not knowing if the time in the water would prevent the rounds from firing. He started running at the fallen gunman, ready to fire again.

As Vail got to him, he called to Bursaw. "Luke, you okay?"

"Yeah."

"They're both down." The second man was dead

and on his back. Vail rolled him over. Of the ten rounds Vail had fired at him, only one had hit him, in the middle of the back, apparently finding a vital organ.

Bursaw walked up, and Vail handed him the other set of goggles. He put them on and looked at the body. "You hit him only once? I imagine that's about average for a bricklayer."

For the first time, Bursaw noticed that Vail was wet and that his clothes were frozen. "You went in the water? Come on, we've got to get you to the car."

The Bureau car was still running, and Bursaw turned up the heater as high as it would go. "Take those clothes off."

"Don't get me wrong. I do find you attractive, but . . ." Bursaw helped him pull his jacket off in the confined space. While Vail finished undressing, Bursaw called WFO and told them to get some agents out there.

When he was finished, he got out of the car and took a flashlight from the trunk. He headed back to the beach and five minutes later returned with a set of clothes. "One of the dead guys?" Vail asked.

"Quit complaining, you dress like a communist anyway."

Vail pulled on the clothes and could feel a wet spot on the back of the shirt where the blood of the second man he'd shot was now ice cold.

IT WAS ALMOST an hour and a half before agents from the Richmond office arrived. Fifteen minutes later

Kate drove up. She smiled at Vail, a mixture of sarcasm and relief. "I thought you were going to call me if there was shooting. And now I find out there was shooting *and* swimming."

Vail looked over at Bursaw. "Snitch. And you still owe me dinner."

Kate said, "I assume that's Longmeadow's remains in the trunk of their car."

"We're not sure," Bursaw said. "They're still processing the trunk. No ID, and with whatever they wrapped around his head, we can't even see what he looks like."

"Okay, let's go take a peek," Vail said.

"You're going to a hospital," Kate said.

Vail gave her a look that said there wasn't even going to be a discussion about it. He got out of the warm car, shivering slightly, and went back to Barkus's trunk. The heavy canvas bag containing the body had been opened up, revealing that the victim's head had been wrapped in some sort of plastic material. Vail felt a corner of it between his fingers. He smiled in appreciation. "It's bitchathane. Roofing material. They put it at the edge of roofs, six feet or so up, to prevent ice-dam leaks. You can put nails through it and it seals right up. When you get it off the master sergeant here, you'll probably find gunshot wounds to the head. They wrapped it around him and then shot him. That way there was no blood, skull, or brains leaking out at the scene. Pretty ingenious."

Kate said, "Do you think this is their dumping ground?"

"Thanks to Lucas Bumperlock here, they knew

we were on them, so I don't know if they were about to lead us to proof of past misdeeds or not. They've been very careful about getting rid of evidence. Sometimes even before it becomes evidence, like Longmeadow here."

"It's still worth searching the lake. You never know," Kate said.

"I suppose so, but even if there are bodies here, it'll only take us back to these two. Maybe we've gotten as even with them as we're going to get."

Kate said, "Luke said it looked like Zogas was supervising the whole thing back at Longmeadow's apartment."

"We'd have to get his phone records and find out who he actually called. Maybe something could be made out of it."

"It's certainly not airtight," she said. "And with all the moles gone, there's no corroboration, so is that it?"

"Let me thaw my brain out and see if there isn't something else we can do."

"I still think you should get checked out at the hospital."

Vail leaned in close and whispered, "I just need something warm and exciting to get my heart rate up."

"I think I could arrange that." She smiled back seductively. "NASCAR is running in Florida this weekend."

THIRTY-FOUR

THE NEXT MORNING KATE PICKED UP AN ORDER OF STEAK and eggs from a nearby restaurant and let herself into the former observation post on Sixteenth Street. The night before, she had driven Vail back there and couldn't help noticing that his skin was gray from a lack of circulation, and every once in a while, out of the corner of her eye, she would notice his hands shaking. Again he refused medical treatment when she dropped him off. She offered to stay the night in case he needed anything, and when he didn't use the opportunity to suggest the ultimate act of warming, she knew that the cold had taken more out of him than he was admitting. At that point she thought about insisting they go to the hospital but caught herself at the last moment, remembering who she was dealing with. So this morning, instead of going to the office, she thought she should check in on him.

She found him still sleeping and went into the kitchen to make a pot of coffee. After pouring herself a cup, she went back into the workroom. Methodically, she scanned the walls to see if Vail had added anything. It didn't appear so.

She pulled over the desk chair and sat down to look at the graffiti-like displays that documented what they had done. As she sipped her coffee, she realized for the first time that the maze of documents, maps, and handwritten notes seemed to be almost an art form. Most of the writing was Vail's, and, like him, it was enigmatic yet somehow aesthetic. With all its charted paths and irregular branches, it was more of a two-dimensional sculpture than the record of an investigation. She took another swallow of coffee.

"Hi."

She spun around. Vail was in a T-shirt and pants. His color had returned. "I brought you"— she looked at her watch—"brunch. In the kitchen. It should still be warm."

"What is it?"

"Something very Chicago. Pure, slow death to go."

She got up and followed him into the kitchen. He got a fork and opened the Styrofoam container. "Steak and eggs. Whatever you're feeling guilty about, I accept your apology."

"Please, no more thank-yous. You're making me blush," she said. "And on the way here, I got a call from the director of the FBI."

"How is he?"

"Unhappy. He wanted to know why we haven't been keeping him or anyone else up on the investigative minutiae, like dead double agents and the shooting of suspects."

"You didn't mention my name, did you?"

"Believe it or not, of the million or so names that have worn a Bureau badge, yours was the only one that came up. He said he wanted to see you as soon as you had time."

Vail laughed. "I've been fired twice—or is it three times?—from this job, but this will be the first time by the director."

"I wouldn't start working on your exit speech just yet. He doesn't like being blindsided, but he probably figures he's not getting his money's worth out of you unless he is."

"You can't bawl me out and bring me steak. It's very confusing. And as you know, I've been sick lately."

Kate watched as Vail ate ravenously. "Then I'll wait until you get your appetite back." She got up and poured him a cup of coffee. "I don't suppose you've had any *more* epiphanies."

"Actually, I did receive a call from the two A.M. messenger."

He had explained his "messenger" allusion to her once before. Sometimes if he went to sleep with some unresolved problem on his mind, around 2 A.M., probably when his body was about to shift into one of its REM cycles, it woke him up with some sort of answer, probably trying to jettison the psychological baggage of the unresolved mystery to ensure a more recuperative sleep cycle. "And what was the message?"

Vail cut off a large chunk of steak. "As you know, the messenger frequently screws with me, so see how this sounds. It starts with the two air force sergeants. One disappeared and one turned spy. Why did one disappear?"

"If we're right about everything, it was because he didn't want to commit treason," she said.

"Correct. So the Lithuanians recruited someone else from the same project. They must have heard about the technology and decided they needed a piece of it to sell to the Russians, no matter how hard it was to get. Do you know where I'm going with this?"

"The missing guy in Las Vegas, Gaston. You think he disappeared because he refused the Lithuanians. And if you're right, they may have recruited someone in his place. There could still be an active mole at—where did he work?—Matrix-Linx International?"

"Yes. And if there is, and we can figure out who it is, maybe we can use him to get to Zogas," Vail said.

"So how do we find him?"

Vail pushed away the food container. "Unfortunately, the messenger is very lazy. He only leaves me one item at a time."

They got up and took their coffee into the workroom. As though they expected the answer to have been visibly written in their absence, they both searched the wall in silence. Finally Vail said, "I'm going to shower. You figure it out."

A HALF HOUR later, Vail reappeared dressed in a suit and tie. "Any luck?"

Her only response was to hand him a printout of a Bureau background investigation.

He read the subject's name. "Raymond Ellis Radkay. Why him?"

"I checked Matrix-Linx International. Maurice

Gaston had a top-secret clearance. So I figured the LCS would recruit only someone with an equal level of authorization. There were just four. One was the missing Maurice Gaston, leaving three. Another left the company before Gaston disappeared, and one was a female. Who, because of the chess club's complete disregard for women, I would assume they would not lower themselves to recruit."

"And that leaves Radkay," Vail said. "Well, aren't you the little overachiever so early in the day?"

"It makes you wonder if there aren't more out there. Ones who were once useful but are no longer supplying information."

"It's possible, but we have no way of identifying them. Something occurred to me in the shower—other than you," Vail said. "Maybe the LCS has found another use for their no-longer-productive spies. Do you remember those Disney stores that used to carry the old cartoon cels? I think it was the eighties when they started springing up."

"Sure."

"They were created because one of the bosses at Disney was checking out some storage space somewhere and found tens of thousands of them lying around deteriorating. Because he knew that Americans would collect anything, he instantly saw their potential. Each one was hand-drawn, a legitimate piece of original art. He opened the stores and literally turned debris into millions and millions of dollars."

"What's that have to do with the LCS?"

"I'm sure our little band of entrepreneurs were sitting around their chessboards trying to figure out how to protect the Russians' favorite CIA agent from Kate Bannon when it occurred to them, 'Hey, we've got all these inactive and low-production double agents just lying around collecting dust. Let's figure out a way to turn them into money.'"

"So the LCS was getting paid by the Russians to frame me and getting us to pay them two hundred and fifty thousand dollars apiece for no-longer-useful spies."

"Literally turning debris into a million dollars. At a quarter of a million dollars apiece, I think the LCS would have given up every one of their lesser moles. All they would have to do was make Ariadne's thread a little longer. So there may not be as many as you would think," Vail said.

"That makes sense."

"What's Matrix-Linx's contract for?"

Kate took the report back and flipped through a couple of pages. "Ground weapon systems."

"Our chess players would know that ground weapons systems would be attractive to the Russians. Maybe they heard about the technology and asked the LCS to go find someone to supply it. And let's not forget that the LCS wanted someone at Matrix-Linx bad enough to travel out of state, where they're not nearly as comfortable, and go after a guy who apparently wasn't interested in spying."

"In other words, when Gaston said no and was presumably killed, they knew they had to find someone else at the same company, and as soon as possible."

"Okay, Radkay it is. But now we've got to prove it. Let's start with his financials."

Kate said, "But if, like you said, the LCS was actually paying these guys peanuts, what's going to show up in his bank statements?"

"Assuming he is the mole, they didn't have the same time and means to set him up with blackmail as they had with Gaston. Therefore the inducement was probably more money. At least initially. If so, maybe it'll show in either his bank account or his lifestyle. You don't commit treason out of the clear blue and say, 'I'm just going to save the money for a rainy day.' You start living for today."

"And what if we don't find anything?"

"One problem at a time. Can you strip the financial release forms out of Radkay's report and 'update' them?"

Five minutes later Kate held up the altered informational release for Vail to see.

"An impressive forgery," he said. "I think we're ready to go."

"Do you want to take your car?"

He looked at her as if the question had triggered something. He went to the wall and ran his fingers along the documents, stopping occasionally to read something in detail. "I'm an idiot."

"What?"

"Every time we take my car, we run into the Lithuanians."

"You think there's a bug in your car?"

"Some sort of tracking device, yes. It would answer how they were beating us to the moles."

"But how would they get it on the car?"

"It was probably easy. They knew we were going to trace Calculus's movements, because that's what they set us up to do. They could have done it any time we were out of the car. The ones they have now take seconds to attach."

"I'll get someone from Technical Services to sweep it." She dialed a number and then asked for a technician. After a short conversation, she hung up. "He's going to meet us at one of the surveillance off-sites." Vail was still studying the wall. His eyes were narrowed in an unusual way. "What are you thinking about?"

"My father."

"Your father?"

"Like him or not, he did teach me how to get even."

THIRTY-FIVE

THE SURVEILLANCE SQUAD'S OFF-SITE HAD BEEN CAREFULLY selected. The neighborhood was a mix of residential and commercial properties. The building was tucked away, down a side street. The front entrance to the building bore no sign to identify it. A driveway skirted the property, and in the back there was a parking lot containing a half-dozen cars.

The technical agent who met Kate and Vail there was a good fifty pounds overweight, but he slid under the back end of Vail's car without difficulty. Almost immediately he pulled himself back out holding a small black box about the size of a pack of cigarettes. He handed it to Kate and spoke with a quick, professional authority. "Held in place with magnets. You can buy these anywhere. Companies use them to keep an eye on their vehicles, parents to discreetly watch their teenagers, suspicious wives to check on husbands, just about anything."

"How is it monitored?" Kate asked.

"If you have a cell phone with a screen, you can load the software into it and you're ready to go. If not, a laptop works even better." He climbed under Kate's car and spent almost ten minutes inspecting it before reemerging. "You're clean," he told her.

"Can you set up my phone so I can monitor it?" Vail asked.

"I don't have the software for this brand. When Kate called, she just said it involved GPS trackers, so I brought a couple." He opened his case and took out a rectangular box that was half the size of the one he had removed. "This was made to our specifications. No connections, no antennas. You can put it in a glove compartment or anywhere else. It's extremely sensitive and tracks in real time. It works on a special network the government uses, so it can't be intercepted." The tech agent then took two cell phones out of his case. "With these you can follow the transmitter." He turned on the phones and walked them through the device's operation.

After he left, Kate held up the cell phone he'd given her and said, "Did you have something in mind with these?"

"Not at the moment, but you know how boys need their toys. We find them reassuring. If I'd had this on the enemy's car last night, I probably wouldn't have had to go swimming."

Vail handed the LCS's device back to the tech agent. "Put it back under my car." Kate looked at him questioningly. "I'll leave it at the off-site and we'll drive yours. If we turn it off, they'll know we found it."

After dropping off Vail's car, they drove to Radkay's bank in northwest D.C. When they arrived, Kate went in with the altered release forms while Vail called the radio room and had them query what kind of cars Raymond Radkay drove. There was only one—a Jaguar XKR. Vail didn't know much about luxury cars, but he had always coveted the Jaguar XKE, first manufactured in the sixties, an exquisite piece of sculpture that also happened to be an automobile. He occasionally checked on the Jaguar's new models to see if the manufacturer had come to its senses and started building the sleek torpedo again.

According to the rest of Radkay's FBI background investigation, he was a computer engineer with Matrix-Linx International and made sixty-eight thousand dollars a year. Give or take a few options, that was about the cost of the XKR. Vail asked the radio-room operator to determine when it was first registered. A few seconds later, he was told that the vehicle was first registered, apparently new, last June, two months after Radkay's co-worker, Maurice Gaston, had disappeared into the Nevada sunset.

Kate came out and got in. "Since last June he's had a couple of eight- to nine-thousand-dollar deposits in his checking account. He also started renting a safe-deposit box six months ago."

"The LCS must have handouts telling these guys what to do with their money. He also bought a sixty-thousand-dollar car last June."

"I guess we should get a court order for the box," Kate said.

"Actually, with you so blatantly altering that release form, it all becomes fruit of the poisonous tree."

"You did this on purpose so we'd have no choice but to go and confront him, didn't you?"

"You give me too much credit. It doesn't really

matter if we get into that box. The most he's going to have in there is unexplained cash. That hardly makes him a spy. Don't forget that when we found incriminating evidence in a box before, Calculus had left it for us. We've got to get our hands on this guy and turn him."

"And how are you going to do that?"

"I'll let him know that all I have to do is get that GPS the Lithuanians are tracking me with to within a hundred yards of him and he's dead. The choice is relatively simple: a little time in prison for spying or forever in the great darkness beyond. We'll get Luke and go out to his house tonight."

"So that's your master plan? You're going to threaten his life."

"I'm a man of limited imagination."

IT WAS DARK before the three agents got to Raymond Radkay's home in Coral Hills, Maryland. Bursaw drove his car, and Kate and Vail rode together in hers.

Radkay's house was at the end of a cul-de-sac in a new housing development. Although there were several others under construction, his was the only one that had been completed. Vail pulled over in front of one of the partially built residences. "The lights are on, so it looks like he's home," Vail said on the radio.

Bursaw asked, *"So how do you want to do this?"*

"You and Kate wait in your car. I think this will go better if I talk to him alone. I don't want him to get the feeling we have to gang up on him to get his cooperation. See if you can find a discreet place to watch from. Let me know if you see anyone coming our way."

"This house behind me has the garage roughed in. I'll pull in there." Kate got out of Vail's car and into Bursaw's.

Vail pulled into Radkay's driveway and got out, watching the windows. He walked up the stairs and rang the bell. After a few seconds, a man in his late thirties opened the door. "Can I help you?"

"Raymond Radkay?"

"Yes."

Vail opened his credentials with a certain amount of authority, indicating that everything Radkay was about to be asked was merely a formality—the FBI already knew the answers.

"Come in." The engineer stepped back uneasily, and Vail could see that he suspected the reason for the visit.

They went into the living room, and Vail took a seat on the couch while Radkay sat down on a recliner opposite him. "Does this have anything to do with my security clearance?"

Vail laughed condescendingly. "Come on, Ray. The weapons information passed along. The only question I have is how much you knew about Maurice Gaston's murder."

"What are you talking about?"

"The Jag, the safe-deposit box, this house. We know about you and the Russians. And the Lithuanians," Vail bluffed. "Your reaction right now—it's obvious you realize why I'm here. I'm not going to waste my time. I'm giving you a chance to talk to me before we come back for you, and then it'll be too late." Radkay remained silent, and Vail could see the cold logic of an engineer taking over, analyzing his options. "If you tell us about the Lithuanians, we can make your life a whole lot simpler. There's a big difference between passing along a little technology for a few bucks and being an accessory to murder."

Radkay said, "Would it do any good for me to ask for a lawyer?"

"I don't think you were involved in the murder, but do what you want. If you call a lawyer, he's going to instruct me to leave." Vail stood up. "And when I do, so does this offer. Then we'll lump you in with the Lithuanians and you can defend yourself on the murder charges."

"Okay, okay. What do you want to know?"

Vail sat back down. "First, tell me how you were recruited."

"I was approached at my apartment one night. They offered me a hundred thousand dollars if I accepted. It was paid the next day, and I was told there would be plenty more. Two days later I gave them a dozen documents, mostly technical data and schematics. As soon as I did, they demanded to know when I could get more. I knew then that I had made the mistake of my life. They told me that they had video recordings of our exchanges, and if that wasn't convincing enough, they asked me if I wanted to end up like Maury Gaston. I had never associated his disappearance with what I was doing. I knew right then he was dead. It scared the hell out of me. After that their demands were relentless. Believe it or not,

I'm relieved. When you introduced yourself, I knew that one way or the other the nightmare was over."

"It may not be as bad as you think. You have one very large bargaining chip at your disposal—we're going to need your testimony."

"Testify? Against them? I told you, they're crazy."

"The only other option is prison."

Radkay stood up. "I need to think. And a drink." The engineer went over to a hutch and opened the upper cabinet. "There is a third option you know," he said, his voice suddenly cold, mechanical. "I could just run." When Vail saw that there were no liquor bottles in the compartment that Radkay was reaching into, he jumped to his feet. As soon as the revolver came out, Vail dove behind the couch and drew his automatic.

Radkay turned and fired, hitting the cushion that Vail had been sitting against. He started to run toward the back door. Vail poked his head above the couch, and Radkay fired again. This time the bullet penetrated the padding and barely missed Vail. "I've got people in back," he lied. "And I parked my car so you couldn't get out."

Radkay glanced through the window he was standing next to and saw it was true about the car. "Then I guess I'll have to take yours." He started toward Vail and fired another round.

Vail realized he had no other choice now. He stood straight up and fired once, hitting Radkay in the chest. The engineer went down, and Vail hurried over to him. Radkay gurgled briefly, and then his head fell to the side, his eyes still open and blank in death.

The front door flew open, and Kate and Bursaw rushed in with their guns drawn. "You okay?" Bursaw asked.

"Yes, but it looks like I just did the Lithuanians a favor."

Kate looked at the body and let her weapon drop to her side. "He was our last chance."

"He may be dead, but that doesn't mean he can't still help us." Vail went into the kitchen and picked up Radkay's phone on the desk, dialing Kate's cell phone. When it began to ring, he said, "What does the caller ID say?"

"R. Radkay," she said. "With the phone number."

"I'll be right back." Vail went out to his car and brought back his briefcase. Shuffling through its contents, he found the business card Alex Zogas had given him for the Lithuanian Chess Society. He also took out the two GPS tracker phones the technical agent had given him and handed them to Kate and Bursaw.

After holding a finger to his lips, he dialed the LCS number into Radkay's phone. "Is Alex there? This is his guy from Matrix-Linx." Then, in a whiny voice, Vail said, "Well, tell him that the FBI was at my bank today. Tell him I'm freaking out and need him to call me right away." Vail hung up.

"What are you doing?" Kate asked.

Vail grabbed Radkay's body under the arms and dragged him inside the room that was farthest from the front door. "Making lemonade."

THIRTY-SIX

AN HOUR AND A HALF LATER, THE TWO MEN THAT ALEX ZOGAS had dispatched from the Lithuanian Chess Society turned onto Raymond Radkay's street. Slowing down, they allowed their car to run at idle speed while they checked the other partially built homes in the development for vehicles. There were none. They switched off the car's headlights and dialed Radkay's number. "Hello."

They hung up, increasing their speed toward the house. There was a light on in a first-floor window. They pulled into the driveway, got out, and walked to the front door. It was locked. The bigger of the two men took a short crowbar from under his coat and placed it in the jamb. Following a short, quick pull, a loud metallic crack echoed through the empty neighborhood and the door was pushed open.

Inside, it was completely dark. Both men drew their guns and stepped into the foyer. As they approached the stairs, a shot rang out. The muzzle flash had been to their left. Instinctively, they moved away from each other, firing in the direction of the blast. They leapfrogged toward the shooter, continuing to fire. Then, during one of the pauses, they heard a body hit the hardwood floor. One of them snapped on a flashlight and saw that Radkay had been hit once in the chest. "Okay, let's get him out of here."

After carrying the body out to their car and putting it in the trunk, they tossed their handguns in, too.

Five minutes later Kate and Bursaw pulled up to Radkay's house in the two Bureau cars, and Vail came out. He jumped in with Kate, who had one of the GPS cell phones open in her hand. "Looks like they're heading for 95 South. Where did you put the tracker?"

"I taped it to the small of Radkay's back. They'll have to strip him to find it. Just make sure you keep enough distance between us so you can't see them. Then they won't be able to see us."

She handed Vail the phone. He picked up the radio mike. "Luke, have you got them?"

"*I've got them five-by.*"

"Just stay behind us, I'll watch the screen."

"*Any trouble inside?*"

"Just picking Radkay up and dropping him while they were shooting at us."

"*I know Radkay didn't mind, but for you I would strongly recommend therapy.*"

The two men from the LCS got in the right lane of 95 South and maintained the speed limit. It took them over an hour to reach Route 30, exiting onto the eastbound ramp.

"*The two last night must have been going to the same spot,*" Bursaw said over the radio. "*Think they're going to that lake again?*"

"If they're not, that means last night was a contingency plan, which would be impressive."

"It would be if they weren't dead. Besides, these people are chess masters—supposedly. Chess is contingency planning at its purest."

Vail watched the cell phone as the car drove past the turnoff where the shoot-out had taken place the night before. "They just passed the lake turnoff," he told Bursaw.

"So far so good."

After another fifteen minutes, Vail said, "Okay, they're turning off."

When Kate reached the point where they had turned, she pulled onto the shoulder of the road, and Bursaw parked behind her. He got out and climbed into their backseat. "Up there by the mailbox is where they turned in," Vail said. "It looks like private property." Glancing at the cell phone, he said, "They stopped about a quarter of a mile in."

"How about getting the Richmond office out here?" Kate asked.

Vail said, "The king of Sparta once said, 'The Spartans do not inquire how many the enemy are but where they are.'"

"And I believe none of them survived," Bursaw said.

Kate said, "I'm calling Richmond."

"Go ahead and get them started this way, but last night it took them a long time. Right now we've got to find out where they're putting that body and catch them doing it. We'll finally have some hard evidence."

After identifying herself, Kate told the Richmond duty agent that they needed all available agents to their location immediately. She hung up. "I assume we're going to surprise these two," she said.

"We'll have to walk in to do it. Luke, have you still got that shotgun in your trunk?"

"After last night I don't go anywhere without it. I also have something else that could prove useful—the night-vision goggles we took off those two. And one more instrument of comfort." All three of them got out and went back to Bursaw's trunk. He held up an MP5 submachine gun. "When you called today, I took this from the gun vault. Not that I expected any problems with you along."

Vail handed Kate a pair of the goggles. "You and Luke wear these." He helped her put them on and adjust the straps. "Keep them flipped up until we get off the road, or the headlights along here will blind you."

Vail took the shotgun, and all three of them started loading extra ammunition into their pockets.

They turned up the winding dirt road, and Vail checked the phone screen to make sure the two men they'd been following were still stationary. "Evidently they're at their destination." He reached over and pivoted Kate's goggles into place. "All right?"

"Wow, yeah, I'm good."

As quietly as possible, Vail chambered a buckshot round. Then he checked the phone and pointed up the road. Quietly but quickly they started walking. There were some stands of trees, mostly hardwoods, now bare. A few minutes later, they followed a turn in the road, and in the distance both Kate and Bursaw, through their goggles, could see a stone cottage sitting on a small rise about seventy yards away. Thirty yards from it was an old-fashioned water well. It had a waist-high wall around it, constructed of the same type of stone as the cottage. The car they had followed was parked next to the well, and the two men were taking Radkay's body out of the trunk.

Beside the well was a small, newly constructed shed. One of the men carried something from it that looked like a bag of cement. Through his goggles Bursaw could see that the man had taken out a pocketknife and was cutting open the top of the bag. He then went to help carry the body.

Bursaw described everything to Vail in whispers.

"That's probably lye. It'll eventually destroy all traces of the body. Let's go."

When they got to the top of the rise that the old house sat on, Vail glanced over at Bursaw, who because of the goggles didn't notice the red laser dot on his own chest. Vail jumped into him just as a rifle shot came from the house, which was now at their ten o'clock. At the same time, Kate dove to the ground. Quickly Vail crawled next to Bursaw. "Are you hit, Luke?"

"Left shoulder."

Vail pulled his friend's coat open, and after finding the bullet hole in his shirt, he carefully tore it open. "It's not bad." Another shot came from the house. Vail called over to Kate. "You all right?"

"I'm okay."

There was a small amount of cover provided by the uneven terrain, so Vail crawled forward a couple of yards to find a firing position but immediately started taking handgun fire from the two men at the well. He came back to Kate and Luke's position. "This is an ambush. They were expecting us."

"How?" Kate asked.

"Probably my call to the club. Radkay would have used a code name."

From a second window in the house, a barrage of automatic-weapons fire ricocheted around them. "I guess we had a wrong head count. There are at least four of them. And they've got us pinned down in an L-shaped crossfire. Right now they can't hit us. If they had waited another ten yards before springing this, we'd all be well-diving by now. In a minute they're going to figure out that if the two in the house can keep us pinned down, the two at the car can start moving up to our position and pick us off."

"So?" Kate said, with a little more urgency than she intended.

"When your position becomes indefensible, there's only one option. You have to—"

Bursaw said, "Don't say it."

"Attack." Vail picked up the MP5 and handed it to Kate. "You know how to use this, right?"

"I fam-fired it at the range a few times."

"Well, you're about to get a lot more familiar with it." Vail started ejecting the buckshot rounds from the shotgun and replacing them with deer slugs. "Luke, you think you can fire this into their car, one round every ten to fifteen seconds? It'll sound like a howitzer when it hits and keep their heads down so Kate can move."

"Sure."

"I'll go after the two in the house. Once I start shooting and moving toward them, Luke, you fire. Kate, you're going to have to move when we shoot and get down when we stop. If you don't, that rifle probably has a night scope along with the laser, and they'll be able to find you. Even though your two targets are at our twelve, you should flare off to like one o'clock so you're not coming straight into them. Then, when you get there, you'll be on their flank rather than head-on." He could hear her breathing. "You ready for this, Kate?"

She chambered the first round and flicked off the safety. "This is getting close to being worse than our last date in Chicago, but I'll be fine."

Vail said, "Luke, you set?"

He rolled onto his side and passed Vail two more of his Glock magazines. "Hands down, this is the worse date I've ever been on with you."

Vail crawled around Bursaw and watched the cottage that was to their ten o'clock. Then he was up, running and firing. Behind him the shotgun exploded, the massive slug thudding into the car that the two LCS men were using as cover, causing them to squat further down. Kate was off at a dead run in the one o'clock direction Vail had suggested.

Keeping low, Vail used the same slightly indirect route, approximately toward nine o'clock, that he had suggested to Kate, running to the stone house in an arc that swept away from both Bursaw's and

Kate's positions. That would force the two gunmen in the house to shift their points of aim away from the other agents, so they could fire at Vail. If the sniper rifle that had hit Bursaw was resting on something to keep it steady, Vail's path would completely disrupt its accuracy as it tracked him.

The front of the house had a single door with a window on each side. The scoped rifle was being fired out the right window and the assault rifle the left. When Vail got to within twenty yards of the house, the automatic weapon opened up on him.

Inside, Alex Zogas said in an urgent whisper, "Karl, did you get him?"

"I think so."

Outside, Bursaw's shotgun boomed again, followed by the thud of the slug hitting the car. Within the house the two men's focus shifted back to Bursaw and Kate, trying to reestablish them as targets.

Suddenly Zogas noticed the doorknob turning. He snapped his fingers to get Karl's attention, pointing at the door. Karl nodded and backed up a few steps from the window and toward the door to establish a better angle to shoot through it. Then he opened fire, expending the entire clip into the door. Zogas had taken the rifle off the window rest and stepped back himself, ready to fire.

A single shot came through Karl's window, hitting him in the face, throwing him back into the wall, where he crumpled to the floor. Zogas could see that he was dead. He backed up a few more steps with the rifle held on his hip, waiting for Vail.

Kate got up from the ground where she had

found cover in what looked like a deep wheel rut. She could see one of the men through her night goggles. She was far enough off to his left that he hadn't seen her yet. She was hoping that Bursaw could track her through his goggles.

As quietly as possible, she walked toward the gunman. But somehow he sensed her movement, turning quickly and firing blindly. She was in the open now and had no choice but to be aggressive. Flipping up her goggles so as not to be blinded by her own gunfire, she quickened her stride, walking steadily toward him, firing two- to three-round bursts. She wasn't sure exactly where he was, so she would have to fire out the clip in hopes of hitting him. If not, she still had her handgun.

The killer fired back, and now she knew exactly where he was. She adjusted her fire with the next couple of bursts. Then, with a sickening clank, the gun's bolt locked back, indicating that her MP5 was empty. But the final burst had found the gunman, at least one of the last three rounds hitting him in the stomach. She dropped the submachine gun and started to draw her sidearm when the second man came around the car and leveled his gun on her. "*Kale*," he spit out at her in a guttural foreign tongue, a derogatory term every woman recognized no matter the language. Her only option now was to try to finish drawing.

Then a single shot rattled through the cold night. The Lithuanian fell to the ground dead. A head shot had blown out a good portion of his left temple. She had the presence of mind to flip down her goggles.

The first man she'd hit in the stomach got to his

knees and raised his gun. Kate took careful aim and fired three rounds into him. He fell back, his legs at impossible angles under him. She went over and checked him for a pulse. He was dead.

The adrenaline vanishing from her body, Kate started shaking and sank to her knees. She replayed in her mind what had happened. At the time, because her life was about to end, it hadn't registered. Now, in slow-motion memory, she watched a tiny red dot settle onto the right side of the gunman's head. And then the shot. "Luke!" she yelled down the rise to Bursaw. "They're both dead! Hold your fire!"

She worked her way back to Bursaw's position, keeping her Glock in her hand, watching the stone house. "You get them both?" he asked.

"Just one. Steve must have shot the other one," she said. "Hold on, let me see if he needs any help."

She moved quickly but cautiously to the cottage. There was a small light on inside. When she opened the door, she immediately saw the sniper rifle sitting on its firing stand at the window oriented toward the car. Vail was kneeling over Zogas's body, searching his pockets. The Lithuanian lay on his back, his chest and abdomen covered with blood. She walked up to Vail's side. "You all right?"

"Fine, you?"

"I assume that last shot was yours."

"Can you go get Luke out of the cold? I'll turn up the heat in here."

"Sure."

By the time she got back with Bursaw, Zogas's

body had been rolled over and Vail had turned on more lights. He was searching the other man's clothing. Kate sat Bursaw in a chair. Vail came over and helped him off with his coat and shirt. Examining the wound, he said, "How's it feel?"

"I don't know whether it's the cold or the endorphins, but not bad."

Vail prodded it a little more roughly now. "Looks like just meat, no bone."

Kate found a couple of clean towels and gave them to Vail. He pressed them against the wound. In the distance they could hear what sounded like a single siren. "Luke, I think your ride is here," Vail said. "Kate, can you hold this in place? I'm going to make sure the ambulance finds us."

Vail hurried down to the road and was surprised to see John Kalix getting out of his car. "Put on your flashers so everyone will know where we're at," he told Kalix. "Where'd you come from?"

They started back to the house. "Everybody all right?"

"Luke got dinged, but he'll be okay."

"When Kate called Richmond, she told them to call me. I've had this thing up over a hundred. I don't ever want to do that again. How about the bad guys?"

"Four dead, including Zogas."

"I'm sorry, who's Zogas?"

"He's the leader of the Lithuanians."

"The Lithuanians?"

"They're tied in to the Russians. I'll explain everything when we get Luke taken care of."

As they reached the house, more sirens could be heard in the distance. Kalix went inside. "Luke, how you doing?"

He said to Kalix, "I'm begging you, John, make Vail go back to Chicago."

Kalix said, "Kate, how about you?"

"You should have seen her," Bursaw said. "Charging the enemy, taking them out with that MP5. It was definitely ladies' night out there."

"One of them anyway," she said, looking at Vail.

"Well, Bannon," he said, "if you think you've had trouble getting a date up until now, wait until the guys hear about you machine-gunning men who cross you."

"Actually, I'm thinking about reloading right now."

THIRTY-SEVEN

THE BLURRY LIGHT OF DAWN HAD COME UP JUST AS VAIL AND Kate started back to Washington. Bursaw had been taken to a local hospital, and the doctor had said he would be fine but that he wanted to keep him for twenty-four hours to preclude the risk of infection. Agents from the lab had been brought in to supervise the crime-scene investigation and the excavation of the well where it appeared that multiple bodies had been dumped.

Vail was unusually quiet during the drive. As they crossed into D.C., Kate said, "You're going to make me ask?"

"About?"

"About searching Zogas's body?"

Vail said, "Yes, I searched his body."

"And you don't want to tell me if you found anything." When he didn't answer, she said, "Apparently that isn't what's really bothering you."

"You're right, it's not. My real problem is that your first instinct was to call Kalix."

"He's the assistant director in charge of counterintelligence. Remember, the director wanted him in the loop. You know, the director, the guy who keeps calling me every time something goes wrong.

What's the big deal? The entire Richmond division was on their way—do you think it was going to be kept a secret?"

"For once let's look at this from my perspective. Six months ago I told you that under no circumstance would I work for the FBI. And then again two weeks ago, I made it quite clear I did not want to get involved in this. But when the director told me what had happened to you, I agreed, for no other reason than . . . well, since I don't know how you really feel about me—let's call it loyalty. And never once did I back off my commitment to you. The only thing I asked in return was that no one at headquarters be told what we were doing. Apparently even after all this time, you don't understand that's how I get things done. I knew they would find out soon enough, but I'd have enough time to figure out the next step before they got in the way. As they did when Dellasanti was killed at the drop. And, even worse, the next day, when they somehow figured out I was going to the park to look for more evidence. I don't know how they figured out what I was doing. I didn't think they were smart enough. But you were."

"You think I told Langston?"

"After this call to Kalix, I'm starting to wonder."

"Why would I do that?" she asked.

"I don't know. I hope it's not because of your career, but that is the one thing that keeps getting in our way."

"So you think—" She stopped herself and fell silent for a moment. "All along, you didn't really care if the director or Kalix found out what we were doing. Your telling me to keep it quiet was just a test of my loyalty, wasn't it?"

"If it was, do you think you passed?"

She laughed sarcastically. "You do understand that the real problem here is your inability to trust anyone. I understand that, because I'm the same way. At least I was. But I'd like to think I've made myself change. And do you know why? Because I thought there was a chance for us. The first time I came to Chicago, that was one of the most difficult, most open things I've ever done. I was hoping that my trust would be contagious. But it wasn't. That's why our last date was a catastrophe. That's why I told you not to come here for New Year's. You can't trust anyone or anything. I understand now that it's because of what your father did. The other night when you told me about him, I thought you were finally letting me inside your life. The problem is that deep down inside, you don't want to let go of what your father did to you. You think it gives you an edge, and I suppose it does. Nothing gets by you. While that makes you a great agent, it's the reason there'll never be any hope for us. You absolutely will not allow yourself the vulnerability that is necessary if two people are going to trust each other. You keep trying to make your life failureproof, and you believe that the only way to do it is to cut everyone out of it."

"You don't think I've tried to trust people?"

"I don't think you've even tried to trust yourself."

"That's ridiculous."

"Is it? You're even afraid to let anyone see your sculptures. Your pieces are good, really good, but you don't trust yourself enough to put them out there. You're one of the bravest men I know, but I seriously doubt that you have the courage to ask yourself why that is."

Vail stopped at a light, and she got out, slamming the door. The light changed, and he sat there, watching as she hurried away.

VAIL STOOD IN Alex Zogas's house, unable to stop thinking about his argument with Kate. She, of course, had been right. He was incapable of trusting anyone. But that was hardly a revelation for him. It was something he had reluctantly accepted about himself long ago. And she was right about its giving him an edge, especially when it came to resolving complex situations like going after the LCS. And also, there couldn't be any argument that he was unwilling to do anything that would take away that advantage.

If asked twenty-four hours earlier, he would have said unequivocally that the one person in the world he did trust was Kate Bannon, but, as she had demonstrated, that wasn't true. Since there was no longer an investigation to camouflage his flaws, he wondered if he hadn't picked the fight with her so he wouldn't have to complicate his life by committing to a relationship with her. Maybe that was why he was now standing in Zogas's house—to prolong the investigation, to delude himself with the possible repair of the impossible rift between them.

There had not been anything in Zogas's pockets except his wallet and keys, which Vail used to get into the house. He turned on the computer, which sat on a living-room table. While he waited for it to fully load, the image of Kate's face, twisted with anger and, even worse, disappointment rose up in his memory. He blanked it out halfheartedly, knowing that it would be back.

To suppose that the FBI had uncovered every single double agent in Washington, at least those recruited by the Lithuanians, would have been naïve and shortsighted. They had given up their inactive sources to further the Calculus scheme, but there still had to be individuals currently supplying them with information. If the entire Calculus matter had proved anything, it was how susceptible the government had become to counterintelligence. Espionage was no longer about one country trying to gain an upper hand militarily or politically; it was about the global marketplace—technologies and trade secrets to be stolen and sold.

Raymond Radkay had existed completely undetected, so why not others? If there were others, their names, addresses, and contact points had to be kept somewhere. Vail started checking the files on the computer. There weren't many documents stored, but he would have been surprised if Zogas had been that obvious.

Next he checked the Internet history. It looked as though the last Web site that Zogas had visited was something called American Business News. Vail clicked on it. At first glance it appeared to be a generic business site, as uninteresting as its bland graphics.

He clicked on the "About Us" link, and again the description was uninteresting, except for one fact—although it tried to make the reader think otherwise, it wasn't American. The syntax, possessive pronouns, and vocabulary contained a few small errors that indicated that someone whose first language was not English had written the copy.

There was a freshly posted article that had been cut and pasted from some unattributed publication. It described a new chemical process for supersynthetic motor oil that was being developed by a company in Maryland.

Off to the right side of the home page was the heading "For Our Clients." Vail couldn't access it because there were user-ID and password windows that had to be filled in to open it. What was this site? Vail pushed back from the table and stared at the screen, trying to make sense of it. He dug the heels of his hands into his eyes, reminding himself how little sleep he'd had in the last two days. To distract himself he got up and walked around the room, settling onto a recliner in the living room. He turned on the television and started running through the channels, using the rhythm of the changing images to hypnotize himself into a brief period of thoughtlessness.

After five minutes he went back to the computer. Looking at the page again, he suddenly realized its purpose. It was how the Russians and the LCS communicated. Both of them were able to access and upload onto it. The Russians sent their "orders" to it in the innocuous form of business articles, and the LCS could send coded e-mails through its "Contact Us" link. But what was the "For Our Clients" section used for, and why was it protected by a password?

Vail started searching through the house for anything that might have a password written on it. When he didn't find anything, he returned to the living room. On the wall next to the recliner were three large picture frames. Each contained twelve postcards forming a large rectangle. On all of them were depictions of chessboards with pieces in the final stages of a match. But there were things that weren't right about them. Of the thirty-six cards, each one had four white pieces and four black pieces remaining. The second thing was that even with Vail's limited knowledge of chess, he could see that their positions of play were not logical. The only reason someone would go to the expense of turning a postcard into a wall display would be to recall the last position of the pieces before a checkmate. As he scanned the cards, he could see that none of the games were in check.

And why were there so many of them? Taking out his knife, he slit open the back of the frames and then slid his knife between the cards and the backing until they came off. All twelve had been mailed from Washington, D.C. The return address was a post-office box. Why would two people play a game of chess by mail within the same city?

Then he compared the dates. Each was marked

on the second of the month, unless it was a Sunday. Of course, he thought, the second day of the month was when the passwords were changed. Zogas had mounted them and put them in plain sight as trophies, proving, as so many sociopaths needed to, that he was smarter than the rest of the world. And shoving it right in everyone's face was part of the rush. There was no way any of them could hurt him once the passwords had been changed.

Quickly, Vail peeled the other cards from their backings and checked the dates. The last was dated December. That meant that if they contained the code for getting into the Web site, there was a card with this month's password on it. But where was it? Vail started tearing the house apart but then realized where it was. And that he had actually seen it, in a different form, without realizing what it was.

He drove to the Lithuanian Chess Society, trying not to think about Kate. He could have called and invited her along as an apology, but it would probably have been too little too late. And if he didn't give her a chance to say no, he could make himself believe there was hope, at least a little longer.

Using Zogas's keys, he let himself in and headed back to the office. The computer was still on from the night before. Vail checked the Internet history and found that the last entry was the American Business News. He clicked into the user-ID window and then looked over at the chessboard next to the desk that Zogas had claimed was for his mail game. The last postcard could be anywhere, maybe even destroyed since Kate's and his visit there. But Zogas had probably used the actual board setup as a quick reference to the codes. Once it became apparent that the FBI was starting to focus in on the LCS, he would have been able to kick it over quickly should there be a raid.

On the board there were eight pieces—four white, four black—and, as on the postcards, the degree of their engagement was illogical.

A chessboard has sixty-four squares designated *a* through *h* along the top and bottom rows, left to right, and *1* through *8* vertically as you face the board. So the top left corner is a8, the bottom left corner is a1, and the top right is h8. Then the rank of the piece is added in. If the white queen was sitting in its beginning position, it would be designated Qd1. If it was moved straight ahead three spaces, it would be Qd4.

To test his theory, Vail had to decide whether black positions were to be used for the user ID or for the passwords. The site could have been protected by a system by which if one wrong entry were made, access would become permanently denied. He took out the postcards he had taken from Zogas's house; they all had the black pieces at the top of the boards. Since the user-ID space was over the password window, he decided to use the black pieces as the user ID. Carefully, he typed into the password box the twelve numbers and letters designated by the four black pieces and then did the same with the four white pieces into the password box. He clicked on "Log In."

A page opened, and a list of seventeen names, addresses, and phone numbers scrolled down. Vail still wasn't sure what they were until he got toward the bottom. Number eleven was Raymond Dante Radkay. Radkay's middle name didn't seem right to Vail. He would have remembered "Dante." He looked at the other middle names, some of which were Houston, Spain, and Opus. They didn't seem right either. Most likely they were a quick reference to the moles' code names.

Sixteen more spies, and no one in the FBI had any idea they existed. Until now.

THIRTY-EIGHT

IT WAS THE MIDDLE OF THE NIGHT, AND KATE COULDN'T GET herself to sleep. It had been a day and a half since she'd jumped out of Vail's car. She got up and opened a bottle of wine, turning on the television. Scanning through the channels, she found a Spanish soap opera, which she couldn't understand a word of. It was the perfect distraction, as it took her complete concentration to try to figure out the relationships between the characters by the expressions on the emotive actors' faces. After an apparent series of arguments over a sisterly affair and the help of half a bottle of wine, she finally dropped off in the chair.

Although she woke up early the next morning, Kate didn't get to the office until late afternoon. She'd sat around her apartment thinking about Vail and what he'd said. By now he was probably gone. The Calculus case was over, and everyone was accounted for—or would be as soon as they finished the DNA analysis of the bodies from the well. She did some housework, vacuuming carpets that didn't need it and pulling weeds in her garden.

After finally arriving at the office, she turned on her computer. Feeling-sorry-for-herself time was over. Back to the Bureau's business. She checked her e-mails, and there was the usual overnight bureaucratic avalanche of meaningless memos and directionless directives. But there was one sender she didn't recognize. It was simply entitled "A Favor." She opened it.

Kate,

Leaving my gun and creds here at the off-site, plus a few other things, if you wouldn't mind.
Also check www.americanbusinessnews.com

Stan

That he'd signed the message "Stan" caused her to smile.

She felt a tear run down her cheek. He had risked his life to clear her, and she continued to expect so much from him—too much, she supposed. Instead of trying to understand his side of things, she'd lost her temper as quickly as he had. Maybe, deep down, she didn't want to have to take any more chances, which was the exact thing she'd accused him of. She wondered if there was any chance that he was still in Washington. The time on the message was 5:14 A.M. Knowing him, she was sure he would have sent it just as he was heading out the door. As much as she wanted to race over there and find out, she had a late meeting. It was the only reason she'd come to work. Maybe it really was time to move on.

She clicked on the link and found the site's generic quality curious. Since Vail had sent it, she suspected that there was more to it than met the eye. It was probably part of "plus a few other things" he'd referred to. There was something waiting for her at the off-site. She packed up her briefcase and headed for the garage.

IT WAS PAST five thirty and already dark when Kate let herself into the off-site. The alarm was set, so she knew that Vail wasn't there. She punched in the code and went upstairs to the workroom. Vail's credentials and his Glock were on the desk in front of the computer. She checked the room that he had used for a bedroom and found that one of his suitcases was still there. She opened it and found his winter clothing. That's right, she reminded herself, he was going to Florida.

Back in the workroom, she noticed that the computer was on. She turned on the monitor, and the Web page for American Business News appeared. The only difference was the "For Our Clients" windows for user ID and passwords were filled in. Carefully, she clicked on. When she saw the list of sixteen names, she half collapsed into the chair. She immediately spotted Radkay's name and knew what she was looking at. Vail had pulled one last rabbit out of his hat, and his message was obvious: He was trusting her with this unprecedented trove of counter-intelligence information.

After printing out everything, she picked up his gun and credentials. Taking one last look around the room, she noticed some new writing on the wall.

Walking over to it, she read:

The Sixth Why
Why would the CIA agent Rellick have to meet with

Calculus three times in exactly the same place and in such a short period of time, knowing that the Bureau was tracking his movements?

What was that supposed to mean? Did it mean anything? Was it one of those philosophical or hypothetical questions that Vail had written for no one but himself? Or was he throwing something cryptic at her, just trying to show that these things were impossible to decode without him?

If there was something to it, Kate was not going to let Vail end this case being one up on her. She walked over to the wall and started reading Calculus's itinerary, trying to find the answer to the Sixth Why.

She spent two hours making notes and cross-checking dates and locations. Writing theories on a pad and then angrily scratching them out as additional facts eliminated them. When she was done, there didn't appear to be an answer to Vail's last question, at least not one that she could find. Kate looked down at the list in her hand and decided that it had to be the priority now.

THE CIA AGENT walked into the airport bar and spotted the man he thought he was looking for. "Vail?"

Vail gave him an appraising glance. "Sit down."

The agent took out his identification and flipped it open. "Where is it?"

"You want a drink?"

"What I want is the list of our European sources that Rellick stole. That is why you called, isn't it?"

"I never said anything about just *giving* it to you."

"How much?"

"I would imagine right about now there's quite a panic over at Langley, so it's got to be priceless."

"Then why do I get the feeling you're about to put a price on it?"

"It's nice to see that the agency didn't send an idiot."

"How do I know you have it?"

"Do you really want me to read it so I can give you a name? Why would I say I had it and risk being arrested if I didn't?"

"Maybe we need to arrest you to sort this out."

"Then I'd use the list to get free, plus get what I want, so why don't I just tell you what I want?"

KATE KNOCKED ON John Kalix's door. When he opened it, she said, "John, sorry to bother you at home, but Vail, believe it or not, has come up with another whole list of moles. And since that's your division, I didn't want to waste any time getting it to you."

"Really? Come on in."

She walked into the living room and sat down, opting for a chair by the window.

"Can I get you a drink?"

"You know, I think I could use one. Any kind of whiskey and water, if you have it."

A few minutes later, Kalix brought her the drink and sat down in a chair opposite her. She took a sip and pushed the list of spies across the coffee table between them with a touch of drama.

He opened a drawer and took out a pair of glasses.

"Wow," he said. "And how do we know these are spies?"

She explained about the Web site and that Radkay's name was on it.

"Yes, of course, how obtuse of me." He continued to look at the list. "Wow. This is going to keep us busy for years. Where is Steve?"

"Scuba diving in Florida—I think. He's turned in his creds, so as far as he's concerned, he's done. I don't think we'll see him again. At least I won't."

"Really? I thought you two had a little more going on than work."

"Very briefly. But I guess it wasn't meant to be. He left the list along with his Bureau property and cleared out of the off-site."

"No explanation, no good-bye?"

"We had a discussion of each other's character flaws that got kind of vicious," she said, smiling sadly. "The only other thing he left was something he wrote on the wall. 'The Sixth Why.'"

"What's that?"

As briefly as possible, she explained the Japanese inventor's process for getting to the root of a problem and how they had used it to discover the LCS's role in the spy ring. "It's called the Five Whys. In this case I guess Vail felt there was one more that needed to be answered."

"What was the question?"

"'Why would the CIA agent Rellick have to meet with Calculus three times in exactly the same place and in such a short period of time, knowing that the Bureau was tracking his movements?'"

"That is an interesting question. Maybe Calculus had to keep checking with him to make sure that whatever clue he was leaving wouldn't cause Rellick any exposure."

"The little bit of experience I've had with counterintelligence would indicate the opposite. Besides, we tracked down Rellick by the phone that he and Calculus used to contact each other. They didn't need to meet. Meeting with your handler too often is probably the easiest way to be discovered. Hasn't that been your experience?"

"Yes, I suppose you're right. I guess I was just trying to play the devil's advocate. Do you think there's anything to this question, or is Vail just messing with you?" Kalix chuckled. "It's no secret how much he loves management. From what you've said, I'm guessing that's kind of how he sees you now."

"At first I thought it might be just that. But once I started driving over here, the validity of the question sank in. If you think about it, why weren't the Russians afraid someone would figure it out? I mean, they met near CIA headquarters at the same park all three times. Almost regimented. Wasn't that the reason you were able to narrow it down to those nine agents whose photos you showed me?"

"Yes, I guess it was."

"It's almost like they wanted us to figure out who Rellick was."

"What advantage would that be for the Russians?" Kalix asked. "Giving up such a highly placed source would be completely counterproductive."

"Maybe that's the real Sixth Why. From all the copies of the documents they recovered at his house, it looks like Rellick's information had dried up a couple of years ago. If they were giving up Rellick, it changed only one thing: Bill Langston was removed as head of counterintelligence because he failed to chase down the connection between Rellick and his handler, Nikolai Gulin."

"Why is that an advantage for the Russians? Langston wasn't exactly dismantling the Russian SVR single-handedly."

Kate laughed and let her voice shift from a tone of curiosity to one of accusation. "Would you say that the assistant director of the Counterintelligence Division is privy to a lot more classified information than his deputy?"

Kalix took off his glasses and set them on the table. He opened the drawer again and drew out a small silver automatic, pointing it at her. "Nicely done, Kate. You walked me right into it."

She stiffened in reaction. "So this was all about you getting to the top of the intelligence chain."

"Sorry about having you locked up, but I had to rescue you and at the same time show how Langston's incompetence was the cause. Nothing personal, Kate. It was all to make me the hero and the heir apparent."

"And that included killing one of the LCS men in that shoot-out when you saved Vail?"

"Unfortunately, Vail saved himself. The guy behind the false mirror was supposed to kill him, and then I was supposed to shoot the second LCS man and switch guns with the one who shot Vail, having it look like I killed the lone gunman who killed Vail. I was outside and assumed that Vail had been killed when I heard the initial shooting. I just opened up on the second man. When I came in, they were both dead."

"The LCS was willing to give up one of theirs to make you a hero?"

"He was the one who tried to kill you at your house by trapping you in the garage with your car running. He told Zogas, who was waiting outside, that you were in fact dead. Alex didn't like incompetence, so someone had to be held responsible. The whole Calculus gambit was his plan. Quite ingenious, actually."

"Except that it is about to fail also," Kate said.

"Yes, I guess Alex wasn't as smart as we thought he was. But he was quite a businessman and recognized an opportunity when it came along. Because of the Bureau's ever-increasing scrutiny of the Russian SVR, it had become almost impossible for them to recruit spies. So Zogas started providing the service. He thought the Russians would be his customers for life. What he and I planned to do in the future was that when one of his moles stopped producing, I would be given the name so I could 'uncover' him, enhancing my reputation. Which in turn would give me access to more and more information, not only within the Bureau but also from the other agencies. I would have become the great American hero."

"How about Sundra Boston? How did you know she was onto the LCS?" Kate asked.

"Every morning I checked the Bureau computer system to see if anyone was querying the LCS or any of the moles they were willing to give up—or myself, for that matter. When she requested tolls on Longmeadow, we knew we had to get rid of her."

"How about the guy in the tunnel in Chicago?"

"He knew that Vail was coming, because Vail had me wire the funds to the account. Vail was getting to be a real thorn in our side, so our man in Chicago was told to take him out. He knew there was no real money on its way. As soon as Vail killed him, I told Zogas, and he came up with the ambush that was supposed to make me Vail's savior. Zogas was brilliant at visualizing and planning for contingencies. Off of the ambush, he had set up the CIA involvement with that phone number that would lead you and Vail to Rellick. I came up with the idea that the Russians were protecting a CIA agent. Then if Vail didn't figure out the three contacts between Calculus and Rellick, I would have. I knew about the video with Gulin and him, and Langston's inability to see its importance. And I knew that you knew Rellick. The other eight photos were men I was pretty sure you didn't know, so you'd have to pick out Rellick. Funny thing was, Rellick had no idea about your being framed to *protect* him. In the end he just thought the government had finally caught up with him."

"Why didn't you kill Longmeadow when we first heard him on that tape?"

"Zogas liked to profit from every death. Longmeadow was in the air force and technically bright. He had the potential to be of use later. There was no need to kill him when you missed him the first time around. The only reason they put him on the list was that when Zogas was putting this together, Longmeadow was becoming demanding. I always knew where you and Vail were because of the GPS in Vail's car. I was the one who was monitoring it."

Kate said, "That's how you followed him to the Maryland park when he found the flash drive."

"Yes."

"And what about you? What did you do it for? Idealism? No, that's never really the case, is it? Was it to make fools of everyone else?"

"I suppose that was part of it, but ultimately it was about one million dollars a year, tax free."

"And now?"

"I'll have to defect. I will be looked up to in Russia—not that it's a big deal, but at least I won't be spending the rest of my life in prison. And I have three million dollars in an account there. It's like an SVR 401(k)."

"More likely you'd be looking at the death penalty."

"If you're trying to get me to surrender, Kate, your salesmanship could use a little work. However, the point is moot, since I'm holding the gun," Kalix said. "But I do have one question: How did Vail break the Web site's code? I have a different access code than Zogas did, but they're the same number of digits, twenty-four. The Russians said they're uncrackable. There are over eighty million combinations. And they change the codes every month."

"I have no idea, but maybe that's who Vail is, one in eighty million."

"Too bad he's not around to save you this time."

"So what are you going to do, John?"

"You don't think I would have given you all the answers and then let you live, did you?"

"Then I've got some bad news for you." She unbuttoned the top two buttons on her blouse, revealing a transmitter mike taped under her bra.

Kalix tightened his grip on the automatic. "How do I know that's not a bluff?"

"Why do you think I sat down in front of the windows? There's a SWAT team out there with a sniper locked onto you."

He smiled cautiously. "You've learned a lot of tricks from Vail. This feels like one of his bluffs."

"It could be."

"Then I assume there's a green-light word or phrase for him to fire. What is it?"

"Think about it for a second. If I say it, you're dead."

Kalix took a moment. "Kate, one of us isn't walking out of here alive. If you're bluffing, you're dead. If you're not . . . well, I'm not going to prison or to death row. So let's have the word and find out which it is." He raised the gun up to where he could aim it more accurately.

"The word is . . ." She stopped, looking uncomfortable.

After a few seconds, Kalix said, "You *are* bluffing." He thumbed back the hammer.

". . . John Kalix is *Agent X*."

The window exploded as the shot caught Kalix fully just above the ear, ripping him sideways out of the chair.

AFTER

VAIL WALKED UP TO THE FRONT DOOR OF THE SIXTEENTH Street off-site and, knowing that it would be the last time, took a moment to admire the exterior construction of the old mansion. The weather had gotten warmer, almost springlike. He stuck his key in the lock and was a little surprised when it opened. After turning off the alarm, he took his time walking up the black marble staircase, listening to the echo of his steps remind him of what he was leaving behind. The door to the workroom was closed, and, not knowing what to expect, he took a moment before opening it.

Everything had been taken from the walls, which had been patched and painted. The furniture and other pieces of equipment were in their original places. In the back room, the cot he'd slept on was gone. His suitcase with the clothes he'd left behind was on the floor in its place.

Back at the former workroom, he called the CIA agent he'd met at the airport before taking off for Florida and made arrangements to meet him.

Then he dialed Bursaw's cell. He had called him from Florida after reading about Kalix's death and the subsequent news releases regarding the Lithuanian spy ring. Vail told him he'd be back to Washington in five days and asked if they could have dinner before he took Vail to the airport. "Luke, I'm back. At the off-site."

"Forty-five minutes, okay?"

"We've got one other stop to make, if you don't mind."

When Bursaw pulled up, Vail walked out with his suitcases and put them in the trunk. "How's the shoulder?"

"I can tell when it's going to rain, but that's not such a bad thing."

"That's good news," Vail said. "Do you know where the Oceanic Grill is?"

"I thought I was picking the restaurant."

"You are. This is the stop I told you I had to make."

"That's okay then, because I made reservations at this Thai restaurant that has the cutest hostess."

"This shouldn't take more than ten or fifteen minutes. Did you bring Rellick's phone?"

"It's in the glove box. Why have I been the custodian of that thing? It's kind of creepy, since I'm the one who had to shoot him."

Vail put the phone in his pocket. "All in good time, my friend."

Fifteen minutes later they pulled into the Oceanic Grill's parking lot. Vail spotted the car he was looking for and told Bursaw to park next to it. Once he did, the CIA agent got out of his car and into theirs. He handed Vail an unmarked folder. Stapled inside the front cover was a photograph. "We had a hard time tracking down that phone number you gave me at the airport. Where did it come from?"

The number was the one that had called back on Rellick's phone right after Luke killed him, the man Rellick had called "Tanner." Vail looked at the photo. "This is who it came back to?"

"Believe me, it wasn't easy tracing it back. His name is Viktor Branikov. We call him 'The Mosquito.' "

"The Mosquito?"

"Yeah, from *Dr. Zhivago*. The character Viktor Komarovsky, who seduces Lara and sucks the blood out of everyone no matter which communist regime is in power. The root of the name, *komar*, is Russian for 'mosquito.' That's this guy, Branikov. He actually survived the KGB purges and has prospered. According to our source at the embassy, he's the *rezident*."

" '*Rezident*'? What's that?" Bursaw asked.

Vail said, "The head of the station in Washington for the SVR."

"Supposedly he worked his way up through the ranks by making difficult problems disappear permanently."

"What about the dust?" Vail asked.

"Like you wanted, we had the same source at their embassy start the rumor that Branikov was doubling for one of our agents, a Donald Winston. Of course there is no one by that name with us, but we had someone play the role. We also had our source spread the word that Winston went to the same gym five days a week. Three days ago, when

Winston got back to his car, there was dust all over the passenger side." He handed Vail a common-looking pen. "Just point and click."

Vail showed Bursaw the photograph. "Luke, go in there and get a table near this guy. I want to make sure he's completely alone. I'll be five minutes behind you. If you spot anybody else, give yourself a tug on the ear when I come in."

Bursaw entered the restaurant and immediately spotted the big Russian alone at a table in a side room. He was just finishing his meal and looked hard into Bursaw's eyes as the black agent came into the room, without an employee seating him, and sat down a couple of tables away. Bursaw watched him carefully, because he knew that if someone was watching Branikov's back, it would be at that moment that the Russian would signal him to be suspicious of Bursaw. Instead he resumed drinking his coffee.

Five minutes later Vail walked into the side room. Bursaw didn't look up, letting him know that his target was alone. Vail sat down at the Russian agent's table. "How are you?" Vail said, reaching into the bread basket.

"I'm sorry, do I know you?"

"Sure, you know, Steve Vail. You tried to kill me a couple of times."

"I'm sorry, you must have mistaken me for some-one else," the Russian said. "Someone who doesn't sound very nice."

"You're not Viktor Branikov? Or would you prefer 'Tanner'?"

Branikov set down his coffee cup and leaned

back, a smug grin forming on his face. "Mr. Vail—I assume it's no longer Agent Vail—I have to wonder why you're here."

"You must be pretty pleased with yourself. The Lithuanians had no idea that they were your fall guys. If they'd been successful killing Kate at her home, then you would have been able to have Kalix 'solve' the murder, naming the Lithuanians as responsible, and he would have gotten promoted that way. That was your original plan, wasn't it? Then, of course, you would have had to kill Zogas, so he couldn't involve the Russians."

"If that's true, then you have done my organization a great service."

"That would have been true if one of our snipers hadn't killed your boy Kalix. I don't imagine they're planning any parades for you in Moscow."

"That's an awful lot of supposition, Mr. Vail."

"You're right, and you can call me Steve if you like. Actually, I'm here because it occurred to me that you might have other American double agents left in your stable."

"And if that were the case, do you think I would just turn their names over to you?"

"You just lost a bunch of your assets, not to mention the services of the Lithuanians. I imagine Moscow is not pleased at this point. Let me give you some words of advice—'political asylum.'"

Branikov threw his head back and laughed. "*Steve*, I've come to expect more from you. That's a very weak tactic. One that assumes there are no other options at my disposal."

"Then how about you being charged with the attempted murder of an FBI deputy assistant director and one regular old street agent?"

"I am disappointed. I know this is not your usual profession, but certainly you've heard of diplomatic immunity. If you could prove anything, which I don't see how you can, at most I would be sent back to Moscow. And that is kind of an honor for a man in my field."

"Unfortunately, I believe you're right." The waiter brought the check, and Vail grabbed it. "Allow me. Never let it be said that I'm not a gracious loser." He gave the waiter a credit card.

"You're too kind." Branikov sipped his coffee in silence, studying Vail until the waiter brought back the charge slip and the card.

"I guess you'd better hope that nothing happens to the rest of your sources, because Moscow might start to wonder if you turned."

"I'll try to be careful," Branikov said, his tone amused and patronizing.

Vail looked at the bill and then took out the pen the CIA agent had given him. As he started to write in the waiter's tip, the pen slipped from his hand and fell to the floor. Vail bent over and picked it up. Outside the Russian's line of vision, he pushed the clicker, silently discharging a mist of the ultraviolet powder, covering Branikov's shoes. Vail straightened up and attempted to write with the atomizer pen and then took the waiter's pen and signed the receipt.

"Thank you, Steve. You know, it's too bad you don't do this for a living. It would have made life infinitely more interesting to have you around."

Branikov got up and walked out, giving Bursaw a last hard look.

A few minutes later, Vail and Bursaw walked out into the parking lot and over to the CIA agent's car. Vail took out Rellick's phone and handed it to him.

"That's it? He loaded it into his phone?" the agent asked.

"The list is in there."

"And you didn't read it."

"It's no longer any of my business, so no."

"We appreciate it," the agent said, and got back into his car. The two men watched him pull out of the lot before getting back into theirs.

Bursaw said, "Okay, I'm just a common street agent, incapable of understanding the subtleties of counterintelligence. What just happened?"

"Branikov was responsible for everything. He's the one who contracted the LCS to carry out Kate's 'suicide.' But between our being unable to prove it and his diplomatic immunity, he was going to get away with everything. You know how I feel about that. So before I left for Florida, I asked the CIA to identify the phone number that called Rellick's phone that night in the park. I knew that they had a source in the Russian embassy, because they gave us some information from him early on in the Calculus case. So when they identified Branikov as Rellick's handler, they had their source in the embassy leak it out that Branikov was a double agent and that he was being handled by a fictitious CIA officer named Donald Winston, and that he went to the gym every day. A technique they commonly use is spy dust. When they know their suspected man's contact—in this case Winston—they find a way to put dust in his car and then discreetly keep checking Branikov's clothing to see if it shows up. If it does, they know that he's been in the car and doubling. Three days ago the CIA found the dust in *Winston's* car. So they collected it and loaded it into the pen, which I just used to spray Branikov's shoes with."

"So they're already suspicious of him, and when they find the dust on his shoes, they'll start putting him through the grinder."

"I can't speak for Russian bureaucracy, but that's the way it looks on the drawing board. And as soon as the Bureau starts making arrests off the lists that were in Zogas's computers, Branikov's looking at some serious gulag time. At best."

Bursaw laughed. "It does have a nice symmetrical irony to it, since the dust was part of Kate's frame. Like the Bible says: 'Dust to dust.'"

"I think the thing I like best about you, Luke, is you appreciate just how flawed an individual I am."

"That's very flattering—I think—but you're still buying dinner."

"Let's go meet your Thai hostess."

They drove for a while before Bursaw asked, "Well, how was wreck diving?"

"It was okay, you know."

"I never really take vacations, but aren't you supposed to look at least a little bit happy when you come back?"

"Sounds like I'm about to be the recipient of well-intentioned but pointless meddling," Vail said.

"As a friend it's my job to stick my nose in your business."

"Right now that would be a good way to end our friendship."

"Okay, what do you want to talk about?"

"Catch me up on what's been going on since I left."

"We found six bodies in the well. They've only been able to identify two of them—Sundra and that missing air force sergeant. The lye had been working on the others for a while, so we may never know who they are."

"And what are you doing with all your free time now?"

"I do have one fairly large bone to pick with you. They've got me working counterintelligence because I know all the players, and thanks to you they figure I can keep my mouth shut."

"Glad to help."

"Actually, it's not that bad. We're going after guys we know are spies. It's not like the rest of the time where you're guessing and hoping. And if I get bored, I'll do something not so surprisingly stupid and be sent back to WFO. You know me, whatever way the wind blows."

"For someone with a degree in philosophy, you have an extraordinary lack of it in your personal life."

"Said the bricklayer with a master's degree."

Vail smiled. "It's like that old Bureau adage, 'If you want something done right, go find yourself a misfit.'"

Bursaw watched the street in front of him for a few blocks before saying, "So you're not going to ask?"

Vail looked at him and then went back to staring out the windshield. "Okay, how is she?"

"Was that so hard?" Bursaw demanded.

"Don't press your luck. How is she?"

"You would think with all the press she's gotten for taking down the LCS and cleaning up the little problem inside our own hallowed halls, she'd be on top of the world, but I think her face is at least as long as yours. You should try to see her before you go."

"I gave that a lot of thought when I was gone. I think we're both too comfortable with being mildly unhappy. It precludes unhappiness on a larger scale."

"And you talk about my personal philosophy being misguided."

"Ironic, isn't it? The thing that brought Kate and me together is what ultimately keeps us apart. We're a great match working together, and the little time spent completely away from the job has been very good, but invariably her work creeps back in and that's the end of it."

"She told me how this case has gotten in the way. Not that she had to tell me how you are. But it's over now. I don't have all the particulars, but knowing you, I'm going to guess it's long past your turn to blink."

"I said some things that would be hard for her to forgive. She'll be better off if I just get out of here."

"And how would you be?"

Vail stared at him for a few moments. "You're a good friend, Luke."

Bursaw pulled in to a parking space. "In all the

time I've known you, I've never seen anyone change your mind, so I'm done trying." He turned off the engine. "Let's eat."

As Vail got out of the car, he realized that they were in the section of Georgetown where he and Kate had gone to dinner the night they'd arranged her escape. He and Bursaw walked into the same small courtyard where they had window-shopped. It was late enough that all the stores were closed but one. Vail glanced into the window of the art gallery where he and Kate had stood that night when he told her about his father.

There were four new sculptures, a series, depicting the same woman in varying poses, all draped with sheer fabric that was somehow more sensuous than if she'd been nude. Three of them had Sold signs placed next to them. "What the—" Vail looked back for Bursaw, hoping that his friend could answer the incomplete question, but he had already gone inside the gallery. Vail looked at the sculptures again to see if he was imagining things. They were his.

He looked past the display and could see some of the people inside, glasses of wine in their hands, Bursaw now among them, shaking hands with an older woman and accepting a drink from a server.

Vail took a step back and, with attempted objectivity, judged the pieces. Were they good enough? He went inside to find out.

The gallery was deceptively large, consisting of three rooms. Other pieces of his were exhibited on pedestals, more than a dozen. He started over to

Bursaw and was about to pull him aside when his friend held up his hands, indicating it wasn't his doing. He then pointed back at the office door. It was open, and Vail could now see Kate sitting alone. When she spotted Vail, she stood and smiled with a hint of uncertainty.

He entered the office, and all he could say was "How?"

She took his hand. "A Bureau plane. Your building manager remembered me and let me in. A lot of bubble wrap. It wasn't really that hard. The only difficult part was taking the chance that you wouldn't hate me for doing this."

"As far as surprises go, this isn't bad."

"Then you're not mad at me?"

He smiled reflectively. "I haven't gotten that far yet."

"The gallery owner thinks I'm your manager, so don't tell him what I really do. He loves that you're a bricklayer. He keeps telling everyone that you're just like Rodin. I suppose you know he was a bricklayer before he became famous. Some of them have already sold. I let him set the prices. I hope that's okay."

Vail, looking as confused as she'd ever seen him, turned around and watched the people examining his work. He turned back to her, still unable to answer.

"*Is* it all right?" she asked.

"I don't know what to say."

"Just say it's okay."

"I'm talking about you. The way I was to you— why would you do this for me?"

"I'll leave the obvious answer to that limited imagination of yours, bricklayer. And let's not forget the way I was to you. I accused you of not being able to trust anyone, and then you left me all the answers. And never once looked back. Of the good and bad we've traded, I'd say I got the better of the deal." She took a sip of her wine. "That last why had me for a while. Only after I left the off-site and was on my way to give Kalix the list of spies did I realize that you were pointing at him. But you evidently had enough confidence in me that I'd figure it out. Thank you."

"I'm the one who should be thanking you. For the first time since I was a kid, I feel like I'm connected to someone."

She put her arms around his waist. "And now I believe I owe you one New Year's Eve."

Vail glanced out into the gallery and closed the office door quickly.

Kate said, "Actually, I was thinking more like at my place."

"Do you know who just walked in?"

"Who?"

"Mike, the director's driver, and he doesn't look like he's here for the art."

"Oh, he's probably—"

Vail went to the back of the office and opened an exit door. It led to an alley. "Remember what happened when I let you answer that phone on the real New Year's Eve?" He grabbed her by the wrist. "Let's go."

"They know where I live."

"We're driving straight to the airport."

"Where are we going?"

"Yeah, like I trust you enough to tell you."

She grabbed his arm. "You always did know just what to say to a girl, Stan."

I'd like to thank the following
people, without whom Noah Boyd
would never have been born:

My agent, Esther Newberg,
who never allowed me to consider
failure a possibility

My editor, David Highfill,
who is the best possible person
to be with in the literary trenches

And the rest of the good people
at William Morrow:
Danielle Bartlett
Mike Brennan
Lynn Grady
Tavia Kowalchuk
Shawn Nicholls
Gabe Robinson
Sharyn Rosenblum
Liate Stehlik